Best regards —

Jerry [illegible]

9-25-13

Deadly Politics

ALSO BY JERRY LABRIOLA

–*Murders at Hollings General*
–*Murders at Brent Institute*
–*The Maltese Murders*
–*Famous Crimes Revisited* (coauthored with Dr. Henry Lee)
–*Dr. Henry Lee's Forensic Files* (coauthored with Dr. Henry Lee)
–*The Budapest Connection* (coauthored with Dr Henry Lee)
–*The Strange Death of Napoleon Bonaparte*
–*Shocking Cases* (coauthored with Dr. Henry Lee)
–*Scent of Danger*
–*Object of Betrayal*

Deadly Politics

A NOVEL
BY

Jerry Labriola, M.D

STRONG BOOKS

Strong Books
P.O. Box 967
Middlebury, CT 06762

First Printing

ISBN 978-1-928782-45-2

Library of Congress Control Number 2013930168

Published in the United States of America by Strong Books, an imprint of Publishing Directions, LLC

Printed in the United States of America.

To my wife, Lois,
for her encouragement,
suggestions and meticulous reviews

ACKNOWLEDGMENTS

My thanks to:

—the staff at Strong Books, especially Brian Jud, Dan Uitti and Ellen Gregory;

—Susan Jordan for her special editing suggestions;

—Eliana for her valuable support.

PROLOGUE

This is a book of fiction, but fiction torn from real political and international intrigue. Several points are worthy of mention:

—Every effort has been made to preserve historical facts.

—Nearly all dialogue has been presented in the English language to avoid the complexities of Spanish, Egyptian and Japanese, versus English.

—Most characters have Americanized mannerisms.

J. L.

BACKSTORY

We last heard of Dr. David Brooks in the novel, *The Maltese Murders* (three such crimes); before that, in *Murders at Brent Institute* (two murders), preceded by *Murders at Hollings General* (five killings in and about the hospital).

There followed a 12-year time span and finally we meet up with David again. Many changes have taken place:

1. He has been fully accredited as a licensed private investigator and has practiced his craft on nearly a full-time basis, extending his reach to the far corners of the United States and even beyond. Additional training in forensic science has added to his demand as the leading investigator of the most perplexing criminal cases.
2. He no longer practices medicine but continues his association with what was formerly called Hollings General Teaching Hospital, attending weekly clinical rounds every Friday morning and occasionally serving on staff committees. One year ago, it was renamed The Hollings Research and Development Center.
3. He managed to serve three terms in the Connecticut State Senate, sufficient time, he believed, to learn the ins and outs of political

life, especially the double-dealing, double-crossing, false accusations. Because he had been victimized himself, he'd learned the hard way that such behavior permeated the system. It had provided him with keen insights that most other criminal investigators lacked
4. He has moved from his modest home to a larger one which he shares with his longtime friend, Police Detective Kathy Dupre. For the dozen years they've been together, each has claimed their wedding is not far off.
5. He has continued close ties with Musco Diller, a world-class safecracker and part owner of the Red Checker Cab Company.
6. His relationship with Detective Chief Nick Medicore has remained cordial but frosty.

PART ONE:

SALTANBAN

Chapter 1

Saturday
May 7

The Chief of Police had been indicted, the Attorney General was on trial, and Connecticut's former governor was in prison. Never before had the ship of state sailed such troubled waters, and Dr. David Brooks wanted to make a difference. But there was more.

"When would I start?" he asked during a phone call from an off-and-on but longtime friend and the new governor, Alex Radford.

"Right away. We can't expect you to weed out *all* the corruption around here, but you sure as hell can improve matters. I don't know of anybody who doesn't think all this is just the tip of the iceberg.

"We have a list of some suspects. Unpublished, of

course. Work with local police, David. They're trying hard, but I think they need your experience. And they all admire you. Can you drop by soon?"

David had been a three-term state senator who, a decade earlier, traded part-time jobs at Hollings General Teaching Hospital and at the state's forensic science lab to devote full-time to tracking down criminal elements in the political game. But he continued attending medical grand rounds at the hospital on Fridays—when in town– – and was one of two doctors on the Board of Directors. The other was psychiatrist, Dr. Philip Bennett. David's base pay, slightly more than he'd earned at the crime lab plus expenses, was derived from a special Connecticut State Fund complemented by legitimate but unsolicited honoraria from other states he had assisted.

He referred to those he'd exposed as "scumbags" who undermined the public trust. Once he became known as willing to investigate rumors of bribery, cronyism, nepotism, embezzlement, kickbacks, unholy organized crime, it didn't take long for him to develop a national reputation. It was a reputation that endured, despite the efforts of detractors who disagreed with him on his long-held belief that society's poorest got the handouts, its wealthiest got the breaks and its middle class paid for most of it.

He often quoted Oscar Levant who allegedly said of a politician, "He'll double-cross that bridge when he gets to it."

And in all the investigations, he relied heavily on forensic science principles which had become second nature to him. Lately, he had delved into military corruption and cyber crime for it was in these areas that homeland security could be compromised. And this weighed heavily on his mind.

David worked secretly with a network spread out over the country—his cabinet—and confined his energies to no more than three cases at a time. Well aware that such work had its life-and-limb risks and regularly reminded that the Beretta Cougar .45 in his shoulder holster and the tiny Seecamp .32 pistol in his ankle rig would not be a match for an ambush in a dark alley, he would whisper back to his fiancée, Detective Kathy Dupre, "So I stay out of dark alleys."

There was seldom a day when he didn't put on a jacket to hide his hardware, and he often wondered whether or not those who refused to remove jackets even in humid weather also carried loaded pistols.

The call from Radford had taken him by surprise, both by the nature of the request and the opportunity he never thought would arrive. Yet on his home turf, locking heads was one thing; bruising was quite another. One would have thought he'd rather take on a challenge in Ohio or Montana than in his own state where he might very well implicate some old acquaintances. *But become disturbed over that?* Such a possibility ranked below zero compared to settling the score with certain politicians who had betrayed him in his quest for higher office decades before. The same ones who believed that selling their souls came with the offices they held. In fact, some had conspired against him in a systematic way—doing their last minute "about-face" several times over. And back then, an unsuspecting and trusting candidate never imagined such deceit would be repeated. If such individuals were on the governor's list, bruising was fair game. Besides, those old acquaintances had long since been moved aside by learned scholars and law enforcement acquaintances, so David had no reservations about doling out what he thought was deserved. A matter of "getting even". Only this time with the law fully on his side.

Kathy was forever reminding him that carrying grudges was counterproductive.

"The grudge isn't the important thing," he would respond. "It's the severity of the reason."

David McKnight Brooks, born and raised in Hollings, Connecticut, always had a hankering to improve the political system in the United States. He subscribed to the popular notion that, despite its shortcomings, it was the best in the world. On the other hand, he also believed that a dishonest minority could easily disrupt the entire system, so that from a distant and inconspicuous vantage point, he could easily pick out the shortcomings, even the perpetrators, in a "not so faultless" pursuit.

If a poll were to be taken, most would vote that he looked the part of an amateur sleuth of sorts. Having just turned 50 and a solid six-foot-five, he kept his uniformly dark hair neatly parted on the right side. Only his eyebrows and mustache showed streaks of light gray, a sure sign, he insisted, that he never resorted to dye. He seldom smiled but soft blue eyes made up for it; they seemed to reflect the emotions of his work: uncertainty, suspicion, relief. Even love and hate. And David knew it too, believing it to be a handicap. Hence, the frequent appearance of dark glasses, even with storms brewing or during prolonged indoor inquiries.

He tried to appear more absorbed in conversation than he really was, checking his surroundings instead. It had become routine for him to be prepared at all times, having practiced the Buddhist concept of mindfulness years before as a way of managing stress.

Many commented on his aversion to overdressing despite the season. He preferred tweed jackets and different shades of charcoal trousers. No hat or overcoat in the winter, just his trademark black scarf and leather gloves.

Allowing little time for David's response, the governor briefed him further on the specific problems he'd inherited. He spoke softly into the phone so David would have to pay close attention—a sure and oft-repeated sign that Radford needed help in the worst way.

"So what's your answer?"

"I can be there within the hour," David said.

"Excellent. We're not in session; it's a Saturday and my secretary's not here; so we'll be alone and hopefully undisturbed."

At 11 a.m. and in a driving rain, David swerved his late model Taurus into the massive parking area of the State Capitol Building, hoping the black SUV that had tailgated him for half the distance from his Hollings office would continue straight ahead. But it followed directly behind and once off the main thoroughfare, gunned to David's left, nearly sideswiping him. Both vehicles screeched to a halt, one beside the other.

"What the . . .!" David exclaimed, patting the holster at his left shoulder.

He squinted at the dark and impenetrable windows of the SUV and was about to curse at it when it sped off and around the Capitol.

David took a deep breath before deciding to follow, hoping at least to get the license plate number. All he was able to make out in the confusion—swift, wet and bleak—was that it was probably an out-of-state plate. No doubt New York, but he couldn't be sure. He rounded to the rear of the building but the SUV had disappeared.

He pulled into the nearest parking space, turned off the ignition and sat there, arms braced against the steering wheel, thoughts whirling. The New York case? He was just winding that one down. New Jersey? Maryland? This Connecticut one that he hadn't even started? Couldn't possibly be. If it weren't mistaken identity then, what was the purpose? To scare him away? But from *whom* or from *what* jurisdiction?

Or could it be entirely unrelated to his investigatory activities and instead to his once having been so steadfast in his continuing criticism of the ways medical research was being conducted? But that had drastically changed over the past few months. He hardly ever got fired up over the subject anymore, certainly not to the extent he did about the imperfections of politics.

Yet, he wanted to allow time for the rain to lessen before he went into the building, so he decided to review what he was now calling his "miscalculations." It had always been part of his nature to rehash things from time to time. The good things and the bad.

About a year ago, he'd finally gotten up enough courage to write his first Letter to the Editor about society's negligence in not insisting that universities allocate medical research monies more effectively, and that their leaders allow only *essential* scientific undertakings. A year before that, he would speak about the subject to anyone willing to listen.

And at the time, although he realized it was heretical for someone of his stature to call for a countrywide moratorium on clinical research except as it pertained to newly discovered illnesses, he had never anticipated the avalanche of criticism leveled at him by much of the scientific community. A curtailment of federal funding? The bulk of research put on hold? Nonsense.

He was suggesting that federal grant money be put to use, instead, covering salaries for teams of special appointees, dozens in selected states, and all with special duties.

David was convinced that keys to the cause and cure of most diseases lay already recorded in scientific journals piled high in medical libraries and laboratories around the country, if not the world. He felt that these teams should be charged with collating all the accumulated data.

"They surely should," he had said at one Rotary talk before that, one he remembered clearly. And until he finally disposed of them, he often stumbled on some of the notes he'd referred to during that talk, such as:

> More has to be learned about AIDS or the Ebola virus or even Mad-cow Disease, and maybe even killer bee syndrome, but heart disease, stroke, cancer, arthritis? For cryin' out loud, man, they've been studied to death. Interpret it all as a universal team. It's time to take a breather, step back, see what we got. Except for a few brilliant individuals who made brilliant discoveries, nearly every scientist who ever lived has interpreted his or her own data to a fare-thee-well, but who the hell's

> ever considered the broader picture?
>
> Hey, call me shortsighted or hard-hearted or whatever but, really, dollars are being wasted if we continue on this path. I repeat...what's needed is for a bunch of curious people to take their time, pore over everything that's already been written, and then make some sense of it.

After that time period, he still harbored similar thoughts but had toned down his public pronouncements to barely a whisper. Kathy had been invaluable in expressing solid distaste for such rhetoric.

He then transferred his fervor to purely investigative and forensic issues. Plus discrediting the political system. And the public en masse did an immediate about face and rallied around him at every level.

"But that's ancient history," he concluded aloud.

He hardly heard the thunder clap or noticed a lightening flash as he raised the collar of his London Fog, but neglected to button it. He exited the car and followed along its side with his hands until he reached the trunk. He removed a small umbrella which he finally located between boxes of debris and documents, then walked slowly toward the rear entrance of the building, his mind focused on the twin concerns of the mysterious SUV and the governor's proposition.

Just inside the massive oak double doors, David stood motionless, scanning the changes: gold furnishings, ornate staircases, massive ceiling-high flower vases, more mirrors, bronze statues of several former governors. Yet the distinctive musty odor hadn't changed and seemed to resurrect the days he'd all but forgotten, or at least repressed. The six years that had started a political journey of ups and downs, of perfunctory promises, of a few triumphs but many setbacks.

A security guard, another old friend, walked toward him smiling. They shook hands and exchanged pleasantries.

"The governor told me you'd be here," the guard said. "He's upstairs waiting."

"Good," David replied. "Haven't seen him in nearly a year."

"I remember seeing you here when he took his oath of office."

David nodded.

On the third floor, he passed through an anteroom and headed toward the governor's office. The entire anteroom was wainscoted and topped with walls that should have been lighter in color but were painted a dark mahogany. There were more internal doors than there were framed photographs on the walls. The furniture was compatibly dark: the usual desks, easy chairs in brown leather, side tables, lighted floor lamps to complement the single large chandelier in its center.

At the chief executive's office door, he knocked softly and walked in. The room looked deserted but something was amiss near the far wall. *Why was the governor's chair overturned? Directly behind, why was a balcony door wide open on a rainy day?* David got his answers when he edged around the desk. The slight body of Governor Radford lay on the floor, crumpled sideways. The ornate handle of a dagger was lodged in his upper left chest.

Chapter 2

Incredulous and deeply saddened, David was nonetheless tempted to perform an initial forensic examination like the ones he'd performed hundreds of times before. Instead, he immediately left the scene to report the crime to the security guard, who didn't bother to check on the body upstairs.

Phone calls were made and from that point on, David had never witnessed so many people converging so fast on the capitol building: local and state police, television crews, newspaper and radio reporters, forensic experts, politicians, even some law officials and media teams from surrounding states.

Connecticut's Lieutenant Governor was one of the first to arrive, then the Speaker of the House and the

President of the State Senate.

David had once served with about half of them and his opinion of each was etched in his mind. Some he knew well; some not too well; most he didn't trust. Not even over a nickel. Especially the ranking members of the committees he'd served on: Judiciary; Health and Human Services; Education.

But strangely, it was well documented that most trusted *him*, more so since his vigorous training in forensics and his taking up the gauntlet to weed out corruption on a state and national level. And people forgave him for his rare tirades about the nature of medical research. Thus, everyone in any authority—even the police—asked if he would take charge or at least participate in the investigation at hand.

David wandered over to a corner, took out his cell phone and called Kathy.

"Oh, no," she gasped, her voice cracking, obviously stunned by the news. "I'm so sorry, David. I know what you thought of him—for the most part anyway. I can't believe it. First his wife and now him."

Mrs. Radford had been killed in a car accident six months before. The two women had often socialized before Alex turned to politics, when he worked primarily in telecommunications both overseas and in the U.S. It often took him to foreign markets, times when his wife called on Kathy for companionship.

"A complicated man," David said, "with a mix of

allies and enemies. Off the top of your head, Kath, should I get involved? They're asking."

"I'd say fifty-fifty. Pros and cons, but it's your call."

"I'll probably be a little late for dinner, either way. Bye." He sat heavily in a nearby chair and rubbed the phone's mouthpiece over his chin.

Lieutenant Governor Michael Burns walked over and, putting a hand on David's shoulder, said, "I hope you'll agree to handle this case. You'll be well compensated."

"Do I have to?" It was vintage David Brooks coyness, sidestepping any financial debate. "I have three other cases pending. Besides, maybe I'm a bad choice. We were somewhat close, you know." He swallowed audibly.

"So I hear. More reason for you to stay on."

"Yes and no. I'd have to *force* myself to be objective."

"Just as you always are anyway."

"And if I were to agree, I'd have to tend to some other matters at the same time, maybe even accept new cases. It might mean extensive travel that couldn't be put off, but that's the nature of what I do." David took out a small calendar from his back pocket. "In fact, as it now stands, I wouldn't be able to devote full time to this case for at least a week or ten days. And who knows: it might be solved by then."

He rose and paced away from Burns, then abruptly returned and, as if announcing the decision of a lifetime, indicated he preferred to take total charge of the case, not simply participating as one of many. Even from a distance on some days.

"Beautiful!" the Lieutenant Governor declared. "When can you start?"

"Monday. Late morning. I have to clear up some other issues before then, but at least I can get things underway here over the next hour or so.

"And getting back to my role: you should be aware, Mike, that I never promise deadlines, meaning I work at my own pace. That gives me flexibility. As I said, there may be other demands on my time, so you …me …we'll have to allow for that. But I'll be checking with the local police as often as I can and, in return, I hope they'll clue me in on anything important they come up with." What David had in mind, at least for starters, was to spend half a day on this new case and half on the other three.

The Lieutenant Governor, still fully elated, agreed with all his conditions.

David immediately demanded that the whole crime scene be cordoned off and that only his acquaintances from the crime lab be allowed within the yellow tape. In fact, the entire capitol building was to be off limits to all but the three from the lab plus a few police officers. It was as if his earlier reservation had never been uttered.

He supervised the photo shoots, the careful removal

of the ornate dagger, the inch-by-inch inspection of the body, the desk, the phone, all furniture and floors in the office and anteroom. Even the fire escape, top to bottom. He asked one of the forensic scientists to examine any nearby parking spaces, despite the rain which, by then, had turned to a light drizzle.

"Any patterns out there have probably been washed away by now, but you never know," he stated.

At one point, he motioned one from the forensic team aside. "Adele," he said, "mind if I ask Sparky, our Hollings criminalist, to join you here?"

"Not at all," she said. "We've worked together before. Great guy."

"And I can't afford the time now or even in the next few days, but I may return here myself. Not checking on you, understand, but another set of eyes never hurts."

"Especially a set with your experience," Adele added.

He then contacted Sparky who agreed to participate.

"Then I'll be in touch with you Monday morning," David said. "I would see you tomorrow but you know those cases I was telling you about?"

"The ones you're sharing with Captain Gilmore in Jersey?"

"Yeah, three of them. I'll just skip down there tomorrow for a while and then have him handle them alone for the time being. He'll understand."

Turning his attention back to the case at hand, the forensics team followed standard procedures in obtaining fingerprints and DNA evidence from anything that he judged important. They took measurements and recorded angles. Even removed the desk contents and placed everything into proper containers to be taken for analysis at the lab.

Only the arduous task of interrogation remained. And piecing together the important triad of motive, opportunity and means would have to give way to determining the most relevant of the three: motive. He already had an idea about this, but adjusted his thinking to focus briefly on the three other cases he was working on concurrently. It would take the greater part of the afternoon plus the following day—Sunday—to put them on hold with Capt. Gilmore's help. He was unsure of the consequences.

He and Kathy spoke little during a sparse dinner, David deep in thought and Kathy understanding it. He did, however, refer to the essentials of what he was already calling the "Radford Business", as if it simply involved one of a litany of cases he'd handled. And he kept muttering the word, "nanotechnology."

The rain had returned full force and noisy, fitting his long held belief that there existed a rain/sleepiness conspiracy. He'd even talked Kathy into it years ago. He shook it off this time, just as she allowed it to begin grabbing hold. But she finally asked, "So what's nanotechnology?"

"What's that?"

"Nanotechnology, if I'm pronouncing it right."

"It deals with things on an atomic and molecular scale. Definitely the wave of the future, but 'tiny' is the word," he answered.

"Like in what?"

"Many things. Electronics, medicine, energy production. You name it."

David went to a window and observed a darkness unusually deep for that time of early evening. The light from two street lamps was finely dispersed and bleary.

They retired early to their upstairs bedroom, leaving a bedside light on. Then Kathy opened up again.

"You've had that funny look," she said. "What's up—besides the obvious?"

"Oh, I guess you'd call it a quandary. But where do I …we …where do we start?"

"Wait a minute. You're including me?"

"Absolutely. Don't I always?"

Kathy rose on an elbow.

"I suppose so," she said, yawning. "But what I don't understand is how did he ever get to be governor? You've explained it before—I mean right after it happened—but I didn't pay much attention back then. What, a year ago?"

David didn't respond, his head still, eyes fixated upward.

"I mean," Kathy continued, "he had so many adversaries."

David finally turned toward her and said, "But also a few well-placed friends with plenty of money. Money talks, I'm afraid. Always has. That's one of the reasons I got out of the game, and thank God I did."

Kathy lowered herself, inched closer to him and whispered, "Yes, but so what?"

"That I got out?"

"No, that he had friends with money."

David sat up. "He bought votes. It's as simple as that. Blocks and blocks of them. You know, bundling and variations of it. You can reward a political ally by giving him or her an important government job if you're elected. But before that, you go a step further by paying guys up front with cold hard cash—the ones who control large blocks of votes, like institutional votes."

"But you've got to get the nomination first," Kathy countered, her eyes heavy.

"Sure. So you pay off the delegates or their families."

David lowered himself back down and after reconsidering, he added, "I know I sound bitter, Kath, and that it doesn't always apply, but it sure as hell did in Alex's case. At least enough to get him elected."

He paused to dwell on his opinion of lobbyists, payoffs and back room deals and, turning toward Kathy, saw that she had fallen asleep.

Chapter 3

By early Monday morning, the weather had changed little, a heavy rain pelting down with ferocious intensity. David showered and shaved and couldn't wait for Kathy to join him for breakfast. Some breakfasts they had! Usually toast, coffee and orange juice. Sometimes he would substitute tea—it seemed to settle his stomach if need be. He settled for tea this time.

He was anxious to share the thoughts he'd stored up during a troubling night but deferred to Kathy's habit of completely dressing up before joining him at the kitchen table.

David glanced at her as she buttered her toast. As was the case on most mornings, he wanted to iron out the pout of her lips with his own and pat her dark wavy hair which was still wet from a shower. And at least once a week, in one way or another, he managed to refer to her short stature in contrast to his. She would place the blame on him, however, claiming his genes "didn't see six-feet-five approaching."

Kathy's high cheekbones and hint of eye shadow always drew his attention. And he would make sure her detective's badge was prominently displayed on her hip pocket before she went to work at police headquarters, thus guaranteeing that he alone appreciated her beauty, that potential flirts would be kept at bay.

"You want me to keep quiet, David, or what? And I hope you take a nap after I leave."

"Quiet? No. Nap? No. I just had a restless night, that's all."

"Yeah, sure. So what's your dilemma besides the case itself?"

"That's it—the case. The Radford Business. Might as well get used to the phrase, incidentally. I have a feeling it ain't going away soon."

He stared at the butter on his fork. "I can't decide on which corporate executives and lobbyists and political bigwigs to call on first. Alex was in cahoots with all of them. Even with foreign countries. Some helped his campaign. Japan comes to mind. So whether domestic or foreign, they're what got him where he wanted to go. It was pretty much general knowledge."

"How about including *former* bigwigs?"

"That's a given. See, the problem is not only the order I'd follow, but how many there are. It would take ages."

He stirred his tea with a free hand. "But the order? Why's that important? Because in the world of politics, whether among elected officials or their lackeys; or in the world of corporate money grubbers; or in the world of lobbyists who pretend to play everything down the middle—any one of them would give the others a head's up. It's like one giant fraternity. My questions wouldn't take anyone by surprise except numero uno. And you know as well as I do, Kath, that the less often somebody rehearses an answer, the more likely he or she gives an honest and legitimate one."

"You'll handle it well, David. You always do. But are you sure you want to take all this on?"

"Yeah, I'm sure." He improvised a grin in an attempt to offset her concern. "We'll see how things go. But getting back to the questioning, I should add there are others to consider, like the staff members at both hospitals." He ran his eyes over the ceiling directly above. "In fact, I think I'll start with them—then move on to the others. At least—I suspect anyway—that the staff people will keep their individual mouths shut."

As usual, their abbreviated breakfasts took less than ten minutes. Kathy rose and leaned over to kiss the top of his head. She collected her purse and a handful of manila folders and headed for the front door.

"Remember to keep me posted," she said.

"Wait. You don't want to read the account of it in the paper?"

"Not now. I'm late for an appointment as it is. I'll read about it at headquarters. Call me if anything new comes up."

She turned once to smile at his oft-stated comment, "I still say you're too pretty to be a cop."

Kathy hurried out the door but returned briefly to hand David the folded copy of the *Hollings Morning Sentinel.*

Once alone, he opened the newspaper and read only the five-inch banner headline:

GOVERNOR RADFORD FOUND MURDERED

David knew the details by heart and looked forward to reading the entire article, but only after sorting out key ideas he had about Radford's rise to the governorship, ideas certain to be covered by the reporters. He put the paper aside, headed straight for the largest room in the house and began to pace, a habit he'd acquired years before. It seemed to bring out the "the most and the best", as he characterized it, whenever Kathy poked fun at the practice.

The living room gave the impression of being overstuffed like its furniture. Every chair had its table and every table its lamp, but gone were the Hepplewhites, Chippendales and the Duncan Phyfe settee that he'd received as a fee for investigative work on behalf of a museum in Vienna.

They had been squeezed into a much tinier room of a former dwelling that Kathy had referred to as his "box", a four-room house where he'd lived a dozen years before he and Kathy decided to live together. Buying a new home was a point she'd insisted on as a condition of their new relationship.

It was a two-story, eight-room Colonial on the outskirts of town, set back at the edge of their property. In viewing the property before sale, the only reservation David had was such a placement on the lot. The living room's French doors opened to neither lawn, trees nor garden but to a waste-high stonewall.

"We could put a row of flower pots on it," Kathy had said. Which they did.

But the front lawn measured nearly an acre, a vast variety of shrubs and overhanging oaks, elms and white birches making it appear smaller. Except when David was mowing it. Because of his many absences, that was rare, and a professional arborist tended to most of the property's maintenance, although David insisted on playing a small role: selected planting. He tried to plant in bold curves, avoiding straight lines whenever possible. When asked about the technique, his answer was always the same: "This allows you to create a mystery as to what lies around the curve."

As he paced, the question of motive again surfaced and he began to review what had transpired between Hollings General Hospital and Bowie Hospital across town in recent years. Would that figure into why Radford was killed? David wanted to fill in the blanks of what he was certain the newspaper would cover, blanks that arose in his confidential conversations with Radford before he was elected governor.

Since the murders at Hollings 12 years before, the number of patients had slowly dried up. Three years ago, its most prominent physicians, including David, had worked on making it essentially a research center while still retaining some floors as clinical in nature.

But its principle challenges involved stem cell research, nanotechnology, gene mapping and organ transplantation, all compatible with his thinking on "essential scientific undertakings." In its strained relationship with Bowie, the two hospitals became a consortium of sorts but everyone knew that Hollings called the shots, which most seasoned Bowie staff members resented.

Simply put, Hollings had undergone a renovation to justify its newly formed name: The Hollings Research and Development Center. All this required approval of a state committee headed by an old crony of Radford.

And there had to be considerable funding from an outside source, in this case from a European company based in Gibraltar. Alex Radford obviously had close ties with the company when he worked for its telecommunications division. The company, called "Communications Plus" (CP for short) also dealt with medical cybernetics. The president and C.E.O. was one Juan Carlos Saltanban, an old nemesis of David who had lost track of him until Radford had moved to an area close to the Rock of Gibraltar. Saltanban had previously been the president of Radonia, a small country in South America.

The Saltanban-Radford connection was one that David and Alex often argued about. And every so often, Kathy would resurrect the many confrontations both she and David had with Saltanban.

David hardly knew what cybernetics was, let alone medical cybernetics!

The deal was that CP would supply the funding for the new Hollings Center in exchange for its purchasing from CP all ongoing surgical and "other supplies", the latest X-ray, MRI and ultrasound equipment, and state-of-the-art devices used in cardiac rehabilitation. But not only that—CP expected Hollings and particularly Alex Radford to pressure other Connecticut medical facilities to do the same. The "other supplies" included everything from DNA–sequencing machines to new smart phones for all employees, plus the switchers and routers that would form the backbone of the state's medical communications network.

In addition, Saltanban expected Radford to influence

other Connecticut communities to have their police, fire and public works departments reband their radio systems—making the switch from analog to digital. CP would supply all necessary hardware and software at a specified cost to each community.

Despite frequent rifts between David and Radford, they had kept in touch.

One of the issues that caused a several year estrangement was their divided opinion about the importance of nanotechnology, the hot new science story of a decade before. It wasn't until Radford sent David a *Wall Street Journal* article about it and until David researched its contents that they once again shared common ground. One section read:

> Nanoculture: one of the truths of [technology] is that revolutions take longer than predicted, but they arrive sooner than we are prepared for them. That is the case with nanotechnology… .
>
> Though it has largely disappeared from the front pages, nanotech is only now coming into its own. Breakthrough medicines; genetic research; new materials such as graphene (a lattice-sheet form of carbon used for everything from filters to computer chips); molecular electronics (extreme miniaturization, thus super small sensors and other devices); and

> quantum computing (small superfast supercomputers) have all been announced in recent months. Indeed the range of emerging applications for nano materials is so wide-ranging and important that, together, they suggest an impending turning point in high tech as important as silicon and integrated circuitry were half a century ago.

In fact, for some time, David had wanted to be in the vanguard of this new nanoculture throughout Connecticut, and it was this that had convinced him to push for the new center at Hollings.

Now 8:30, he stopped pacing and retrieved the morning newspaper, aware that he was a bit behind schedule. His routine: karate class every Monday morning and medical rounds every Friday morning. His detective work was ordinarily sandwiched between these two events unless it took him to distant locations. Monday afternoon to Thursday night were considered sacrosanct for such work—with one exception: the monthly Hollings Hospital Board of Directors meeting on Tuesday morning. He had been its chairman for five years, and even while governor, Radford had become a de facto member. There was hardly a session when the governor didn't argue with at least someone, even the chairman. So David's typical week consisted of a class in self-defense, continued hospital undertakings and "political" detective work. It had become the rhythm of his life.

The article occupied four columns of the entire front page. He scanned it to verify its accuracy and was surprised when he found no direct mention of a possible motive, though it did allude to Radford's canceling the funding for the new set-up at Hollings. No mention of a reason.

Off to the left side, in lighter print, was a brief account involving David, slightly modified but obviously extracted from larger ones in previous years. He knew it by heart and, this time, objected to its inclusion of the hospital's Hole. Years ago, he had abandoned it as a hospital office:

> Dr. David Brooks, at one time Hollings General's own house call specialist, has once again become a regional and national personality. About ten years ago, with assistance from the city's law enforcement and forensic authorities, including his fiancée, Police Detective Kathy Dupre, Dr. Brooks advanced his amateur detective status to become a fully licensed private investigator. Still operating out of The Hole, a makeshift office located in the hospital's basement, the tall physician who possesses the only handshake that hurts people, the one with real bow ties and an

equally wide, bushy mustache, wasted little time in agreeing to piece together the circumstances surrounding the murder of Governor Radford.

There followed several clipped references:

Age: 51.

Unmarried.

Graduate of Yale University.

Navy veteran.

Private family practice: four years.

Practice limited to house call referrals by other physicians: six years.

Black belt in karate.

Interests: guns, his black Mercedes convertible, Pavarotti and Bocelli music, Japanese culture, flowers of all types, study of caves (speleology).

On page three there was a lengthy summary of Governor Radford's miraculous rise in government, having compiled no previous political experience. But it referred to a vast network of key political and industrial acquaintances.

David arrived at the parking lot of the old stucco building that housed Bruno's Martial Arts Studio at precisely nine and edged his way along a winding path to the front entrance. He carried a leather attaché case he'd had for most of his years of detective work. He had a name for it: Friday. Nothing to do with Joe Friday or Girl Friday, just the day he'd bought it. In it were several rounds of ammunition, a pair of binoculars, a postage stamp-sized digital tape recorder, a Tasar, a small container of pepper spray, policeman's whistle, scout knife, box of latex surgical gloves, tactical flashlight and an extra cell phone.

From a dishwater sky, an incessant May rain drizzled on. The air smelled swampy and the sounds were natural enough, and incessant—recurring gusts from afar, the snap and swish of branches behind him, drips from sloping eaves. The rain itself was now silent. He felt on edge but wasn't sure why, having handled hundreds of murder cases in the past dozen years, some routine, some macabre.

Once again he cursed the three flights of stairs he had to climb. And he hated the upcoming routine at his locker where he changed into a pajama-like costume of black-bordered white cotton jacket and pants, even though he'd done so for 21 years now. A black belt for half that time, he conducted a class for beginners nearly every Monday morning and then refined his own skills in percussive *tae kwan do* combat with fellow instructors: kicking, elbowing, slashing with hands and feet.

He opened the door at the top of the stairs, its laminated glass panel bearing the words:

CHINESE, JAPANESE, KOREAN, AMERICAN
MARTIAL ARTS
BRUNO BATEMAN, GRAND MASTER

Unlike ever before, David had a strong premonition that his competency in karate would serve him well in the next few weeks. Especially the *bujutsu* phase that stresses not only combat but also a willingness to face death as a matter of honor. Such was the respect he'd developed for the spiritual concepts it's based on: Zen Buddhism and Shinto.

He noticed Bruno beginning a class in a side room and waved to him.

The Grand Master interrupted his instruction and stepped out to greet David. "Well, I see by the papers that you've taken on the governor's murder," he said. "What a mess up there in Hartford! But good for you. You can postpone your work here if you need to."

Bruno was nearly as tall as David but much thinner, all muscle and no fat. In his sixties, he had run the studio for half his life and once confided that if it were not for karate, he would have gone into medicine.

"But really," he qualified, "I would never have made it into medical school."

"Sure you would, except for that ponytail of yours." David regarded him steadily. "You didn't have it back then, did you?"

"Of course. It's the seat of my power. Something like David's."

"You mean me? I'd never have one of those."

"No, no. Like in David and Goliath."

Bruno paused as if hesitant to bring up Radford's murder again. "But back to the governor, or I should say the former governor. Any idea who might have killed him?"

"Not yet, but we'll see. You have a hunch?"

"Everybody knows he wasn't well liked and that he bought his way to the top. But that's not the reason for the murder, really. It's because he cut off the money for the new hospital setup. I guess you guys call it funding. So he saved the state some money but couldn't save his own skin." He swept the room with a glance. "Too bad," he breathed sarcastically.

When David's class started, he tried to recapture the sensations that were spawned early each Monday morning: the smell of sweat, the faint talcum taste, the give of the shiaijo mat under his bare feet. But he couldn't get Bruno's last two words out of his mind: "Too bad." And the question about a hunch regarding a killer had never been answered.

An hour later, he took a quick shower and left. The words still rang in his ears and he concluded that he had his first suspect even though the Grand Master wasn't on a real preliminary list.

He made his way to the parking lot and although the soft ground was absorbing his footprints, the rain had stopped. Bits of gray sky showed high above, as gray as something else that entered his stream of thought: would there be a note on the car? It had happened once before and he was ready for it to happen again. He approached the Mercedes slowly, casting an eye in every direction and feeling for the Beretta Cougar .45 at his shoulder.

Indeed, there was a piece of paper attached to a wiper blade! David checked his surroundings again before yanking off the paper. It contained a printed note:

HERE WE GO AGAIN, PAL.
WATCH OUT. MIND YOUR OWN BUSINESS.

His heart pounded harder. We? Again? Left over from last time? But that was 12 years ago. That case was solved. Or was it?

Chapter 4

David had expected to check in with Kathy at police headquarters immediately after the karate session to review the preliminary suspect list he had mentally put together. And while there he would consult with Sparky, the department's criminalist, mostly about his take on the nature of the dagger and what he had found at the crime scene.

But the note on his car had changed things or at least delayed them. His house was on the way to headquarters and he would stop there to reinforce the contents of Friday, his attaché case. Translation: extra fire power if needed.

Soon after exiting the parking lot, what looked like the same black SUV that had tailgated him on Saturday appeared out of nowhere, slowed down after passing him and then raced off at breakneck speed. Again he couldn't read the license plate but was positive it was a Connecticut one, not New York.

Had its driver left the note? Was it, in fact, the same SUV? David was tempted to catch up to the vehicle but realized he was behind schedule as it was, and gave up the idea.

He hadn't anticipated so much happening in the last hour or so: Bruno's disturbing words; the menacing note; the SUV. It may have accounted for his swerving into his driveway in crooked fashion. He returned a salute to a postman across the street and bolted into the house directly to the basement.

There—one of his favorite rooms and one which Kathy called "a virtual arsenal of guns"—he stood for a moment trying to remember where he'd stored a particular one. Misplacing things was part of his nature. Even after a criminal case had been closed, he was a sloppy record keeper. If advised to file away written material, he'd say, "that's ancient history now."

Cabinet after cabinet of weapons surrounded him: pistols, revolvers, long-range rifles, carbines, machine guns, shotguns, knives. All manufacturers were represented: Colt, Ruger, Smith and Wesson, Charter Arms; as were calibers: .25, .32, .38, .45. One of the largest cabinets was stuffed with spare parts and ammunition. Three others contained various papers and folders that had been thrown in haphazardly over many years.

Suddenly he recalled one of his cases in Illinois, when he'd chosen to equip Friday with a Super Blackhawk .44 Magnum. That, in turn, directed him to a corner cabinet where he found the gun. He sighed and put it in the attaché case.

With Saltanban on his mind, he wanted Sparky to review a certain document written by the now-president of Communications Plus, titled *Manifesto for New World Order.* It took more time than he wanted, but he located it in a cabinet and put it in his jacket pocket. Plus a CD of a conversation he'd had with the then-president of Radonia. David had never reread the manifesto, but he did listen to the tape more than once, hoping to gain a better insight of the subjects covered.

At 10:30 he arrived at police headquarters, a modernized building atop a rise in center city. It towered upward into a fading mist, one that fell short of masking a flower garden encompassing the base of an enormous flagpole. Its pansies, petunias and roses stood out, but the tulips were beginning to fade, giving its large bed an untidy look. Other varieties—and there were many—hadn't yet brightened to their potential of blue, yellow, purple and orange. Yet David, a flowers aficionado, still took notice of them.

He remembered offering Kathy some advice when there a week before: to offset the tulips'early demise, add some new color, like a vivid red azalea; a group of petunia seedlings that would spread rapidly and soon produce bright pink blossoms; some purple johnny-jump-ups; and several clumps of clear blue forget-me-nots in full flower. None of this had been accomplished and David reminded himself to mention it to Kathy, but doubted it would remain in his mind very long, so filled with other concerns: foul play, not floral displays.

Inside, he greeted Molly, an old friend at the dispatch window and asked, "Kathy in her office …pardon …her chamber?"

"Last I heard," Molly said. "Three official-looking men just left, so she should be there."

For years, Kathy's office had been overlooked in a renovation program and was simply a sparsely furnished space with little more than a heavy scratched up desk, file cabinet, swivel chair, serving table for coffee and two creaky wooden chairs. All else was kept two rooms away and shared with personnel in adjoining offices: computer, fax machine and copier.

But over time things had changed. All offices had their own equipment, including hers. David paused at her doorway before entering. Kathy sat writing at a large desk cluttered with folders, papers and electronic devices. She jumped when she looked up.

"You're here!" she exclaimed.

"Half yes, half no," he responded and sat in one of two easy chairs at the desk.

"What's that supposed to mean?"

David cleared his throat as if to dislodge a foreign substance. "With the exception of one person," he said, "I just don't know where to start with my …you know … my questioning and stuff. But I put together a preliminary list and I'd like to go over it with you."

"Of course, but who's the one exception?"

"Saltanban. He's the most likely killer."

Kathy didn't look surprised. "By phone, right?" she asked in an I-hope-I'm-correct tone.

"Wrong."

"Don't tell me you're going to Gibraltar?"

"Oh, but I am."

"When?"

"I'll leave tomorrow, right after the monthly Board meeting. Radford's wake's tonight but I'll skip the funeral."

"But what if Saltanban comes *here*?"

"He wouldn't dare. He's no dummy." David reached over and took her hand, rubbing it gently.

"Want to come with me?" he asked.

Kathy didn't hesitate. "No. I'd serve no purpose."

"Four ears are better then two."

"I really can't spare the time, David. The chief's got me smack in the middle of a corruption case." She stared at his contorted mouth. "Really, if I thought I'd have something to contribute, I'd beg off here."

"Okay…I just thought…that is…you got the time

to go over my initial suspect list, minus Saltanban and certain others?"

"Yes, let's do that," Kathy said contritely.

"Well, for starters, let's assume that in interviewing those on the list, perhaps someone might slip up. On the other hand, most likely I'll get nowhere. So in this damn business, I have to start somewhere with the slim chance of avoiding nowhere."

She had heard this many times before and, just as often, had agreed with him. "But first," she said, "about that Saltanban. What do you remember the most about him? That was years and years ago, remember?"

"Yeah, I know. But I also know that at the end of all his finagling, the authorities labeled him a terrorist or at least a terrorist sympathizer. And when he seemed to disappear, he was really a fugitive from justice. Now—**bang**—he shows up in Gibraltar! Just how he could live and work freely there is a great mystery." David fanned the air with his hands in a show of disgust.

"The best I can figure," he went on, "is that it has something to do with extradition."

"Extradition?"

"It may involve the longstanding dispute between Britain and Spain. We—I mean the U.S.—wanted him extradited to here. But those other two countries—hell, they still argue over who has the rights to Gibraltar. As it now stands, Britain does. But it's still a bone of contention. Anyway, maybe because of all the confusion that created, extradition got lost in the shuffle. I don't have a clue about specifics but I'd guess that, somehow, because of the antipathy between those two countries over ownership of Gibraltar—including the Rock—neither one was willing to initiate extradition proceedings."

"So he settled over there with no problems," Kathy said, her voice incredulous.

"That's how I'd interpret it. But let's get off the subject for now. I'll size things up when I get there. Here's the list."

David removed a small piece of paper from his pocket and read from it:

> "One: Bruno Bateman—completely unexpected.
> Two: Alton Foster, our dear hospital administrator. Went overboard for the consortium.
> Three: key staff members minus those opposed to whole idea. That has to eliminate Bowie people plus heads of two departments at Hollings: Pathology and Anesthesiology. In other words, key ones had to feel betrayed. No other way to look at it.
> Four: Radford's opponent in the election.
> Five: The biggie—various politicians, campaign contributors, lobbyists and every other goddamned person in the country. In

the world for that matter."

Kathy had listened reflectively and taken some notes. Finally she said, "I doubt if it's Bruno."

"I received pretty strong words from that guy though."

She cocked her head in disbelief before saying, "We should both attend the wake tonight. It'll be mobbed, but maybe we can learn something there. Then go ahead with Gibraltar. Incidentally, why not have Musco go with you?"

David beamed. "Of course! I never thought of that," he said. "Getting on in years but I ran into him recently and he looks as spry as ever. I'd call him 65, going on 55."

"Worth a try," Kathy said. "He's been with you on so many cases, and I'd feel better if you weren't alone over there. Especially with a whacko like Saltanban nearby."

"A whacko who makes a profit."

Sparky's office and lab were four doors away. David hadn't been there since they were enlarged by including the next two rooms, previously reserved for storage.

At a new double door he paused in amazement at the extent of the change. He then wended his way past benches of, on one side: flasks, Bunsen burners, beakers, test tubes, petri dishes, glass tubing, hot plates, and the like—and on the other side: computers, microscopes, two short-wave radios, distillation apparatus, incubators, a digital fingerprint machine, and even a DNA analyzer.

At the far end, Sparky was seated at his desk, arms folded, thinking. David dispensed with any greeting.

"So you finally got the analyzer, I see," he said.

The criminalist smiled, rose and extended a hand which David shook. "Yes. Took some time, but here it is. I don't have to send out so many specimens now."

Sparky hadn't changed much in the past decade, now a fifty-some-odd throwback to a Western Union clerk in a 1940's B movie: slicked-down graying black hair parted in the middle, wire-framed glasses, gartered shirt sleeves, suspenders.

In the past several years, he'd become a well-known authority on how cybercrimes and telecommunications were related.

"So what have you got—anything?" David asked.

"Nothing, really."

"No prints or DNA?"

"None. I assume he wore gloves."

"And the dagger? Isn't that something?"

"I'll say. Never saw anything like it."

Sparky walked across the room, took down an evidence container from a shelf and removed the dagger. David joined him and leaned over for a closer look.

"It's a double edger and I'm sure the blade is 440c stainless steel," Sparky said. "And the gold is 24 karat without a doubt. The fancy design makes it appear shorter but it measures 16 inches."

They shook their heads, eyes glued to the weapon as Sparky rotated it. Its hilt was lavished with silver, its turret highlighted by gold markings and crowned with tiny touches of crystal.

"What do you make of the fancy handle?" David asked.

"Well, I can't make heads or tails of the kind of wood used. Not yet anyway, but I'll be working on it. Checking around in other words. But whether the handle or blade, I can't even tell where the blasted thing was put together. I'd say Japan. But that's a total guess. Or decorated to look like it anyway."

"If that pans out, it's almost as if the murderer wanted to tell us something, mocking us—me really—because he knows I'm a fan of Japanese culture."

"Yet how did he know you'd take charge of the investigation?"

"Beats the hell outa me. But sometimes I think he could be closer to us than Saltanban. You remember him—another cybernetics whiz?"

Sparky gestured vaguely, then asked, "He have any friends around here?"

"Not that I know of. Plenty of enemies though. His screwing people was a hobby, and I don't mean sexually."

David took the envelope containing the manifesto and CD from his pocket. "Which reminds me," he said.

"I want to read you something; then we can listen to a bizarre CD." He hesitated.

"But wait; something else first." He then went into a detailed account of spotting the black SUV twice.

Sparky scratched his head and said, "That makes me think the killer might come from Connecticut."

"Could be, but the true culprit may have ordered and paid for it."

"And that brings us back to Saltanban?"

"Not necessarily. At this stage it could have been anyone from anywhere."

While opening the envelope, David asked, "What about the crime scene, Spark?"

"Not much to go on there. As I said, no unusual prints, no DNA left behind. No sign of a struggle. He was overturned because of the force of the stabbing. The phone was off the hook, probably meaning he was on it when the killer sneaked up from behind."

"Okay, here's what Saltanban wrote years ago. He was the deposed president of Radonia at the time. Deposed because his life became as strange as his actions, which I won't elaborate on, except to say they involved obsessions with telecommunications and cybernetics along with frequent references to super bugs. But most of all, he kept talking about a scheme to be cloned so he could rule Radonia for years to come."

Sparky fashioned a guarded smile and said, "Really off the wall, I'd say."

"No doubt about it." He handed Sparky the document. "Anyway, here's what he wrote":

MANIFESTO FOR NEW WORLD ORDER

My beloved son, Luis. You have received a legacy that I began many years before you were born. Handle it wisely with the skills you inherited from me.

And be careful of ordinary politicians. When they speak, do you not for a moment know they are politicians? Certain corporations try to buy election results and the beneficiaries are favored politicians. If a "good" politician must be good in the art of compromise, then truth, honesty and loyalty are compromised. Contrariwise, if a politician shuns lies, deception and betrayal, he or she can achieve only ordinary status—a stranger to the inner circle and unable to accomplish much. Thus, the stuff of politics is such that it attracts scoundrels or eventually creates them.

But none of this pertains to you, Luis. You are different. You are my son. Be my son. Be strong. The struggle will take years, if not generations. But you will have the temperament, individuality and determination of your father.

Sparky said nothing for a moment, his mouth ajar. Finally he said, "He felt that way about politicians, but did statewide business with Radford?"

"But remember Radford worked for him in Gibraltar before all that."

"So Radford became his puppet?"

"That's about it."

David took off his jacket and draped it over a chair. "Think he's the killer?" he asked.

Sparky shrugged and replied, "He certainly had the motive."

David couldn't wait for his next statement: "And get this, Spark, if you can believe it. Saltanban never *had* a son!"

"Incredible," the criminalist muttered. "What a lunatic!"

Sparky reread some sections of the document, then threw it on his desk as if it were contaminated.

"That's enough of that," he said.

Eager to change the subject, he stated, "I guess Radford blocked his plans."

"If we play the whole thing out as his being our man, I'd say yes. And also that Radford may have been his first big push, financially and otherwise, and that he represented Saltanban's complete failure in a ridiculous goal. But who knows at this point? There may be other Radfords across the country. Across the world for that matter."

David gave Sparky a once over before continuing. "And here's the CD audio. You have a player, I take it?"

"Right over there, attached to the console."

David inserted the disk and they both pulled over stools to sit on.

"Incidentally," David said, "Way back, I got his permission to record what you're about to hear—not that it matters any now. He was talking to Kathy and me and we just let him go on. It's all about telecommunications and cybernetics, which aren't up my alley as they are yours. I'd appreciate your input afterward but, personally, I think it says a lot about a guy who's off his rocker and may have plans beyond what he wanted to do through Alex Radford. Maybe he's already started, unbeknownst to us. And also, see if his speaking without contractions irritates you as much as it does yours truly."

> (David) So before you went into politics, you were in telecommunications. How did you get started?
>
> (Saltanban) It is a long story. As a boy, I was always taking radios apart. Later, I became an aficionado of the history of communications. Even in high school, I knew that would be my field someday, and in the meantime, I read all I could about the history.
>
> I do not mean to bore you but at the

beginning, the first form of long distance was what? Smoke signals.

Then some people called the Sumerians developed the first known system of writing; the Romans started the first newspaper; and the English introduced the first pencil.

Next, the French developed photographs and three of your Americans––Morse, Bell and Edison––invented the telegraph, the telephone and the phonograph. The radio came in there somewhere and I think a Canadian was involved.

As I have said, Samuel Morse invented the telegraph. It was in the early 19th century. Of course it was he who later developed the Morse Code. The telegraph was a very important instrument during your Civil War for both the press and the armies of both sides. And it helped at your stock exchange and at your railroads.

What can I mention about the telephone? Bell discovered it in the late 19th century. And you know, a funny thing. One never thinks of it, but at the beginning, there were no switchboards. They came during the next year. Then

> dial phones, service between countries, and the technology I am most interested in: commercial satellites. Think of these as relay stations that …but I have said enough about these devices. I am afraid I ramble once I begin. Some other time, perhaps I might discuss the radio and the phonograph.
>
> And so, you see, it is all related—all these forms––and all the countries, somehow many of them wanted to—how do you say—wanted to get into the act.
>
> Anyway, my friends, we are now up to the things I used to do and hope to resume when I step down. That is, if I can convince my son to take over as president of my country. I believe the people will elect him.

There was just enough time, as Saltanban was no doubt catching his breath, for David and Sparky to exchange you-don't-really-expect-me-to-believe-that grins. Saltanban continued:

> That is the desire of my early twilight: the presidency of Radonia for my son, Luis, and advanced communications for me.
>
> (David) I'm learning

something here.

(Saltanban) You mean about my son and my plans?

(David) That, too, but I mean about telecommunications.

(Saltanban) Then forgive me, but I shall become more technical. Bell Laboratories discovered the transistor; Xerox the copier; and Corning Glass the first optical fiber that could be used for long-range communication. Fiber optics uses a laser to send signals through glass or plastic.

The transistor, which replaced the vacuum tube, is a tiny device that controls the flow of electric current in TV sets, radios, computers and …but there I go again. I am sorry.

I spoke about satellites already. Telstar is a satellite that was launched in early 1960. It relayed telephone calls, television shows and other communications between your country and Europe.

My company dealt with fiber optics and satellites primarily, but I have recently become interested in cybernetics. In point of fact, three months ago, I completed a book on the subject, and I am now anxiously awaiting word from the publisher. I want to advance knowledge about how information is transmitted by the control mechanism of machines and the nervous system of living things.

(David) Like animals?

(Saltanban) Yes, animals …humans. Yes, anything living. But I believe I have rambled on too long. You asked me the time and I made you a watch!

(David) Nonsense. That was most informative. One last question, though. What about computers? Where do you think they're taking us?

(Saltanban) I am concerned. The Internet with its encrypted messages can be such a tool of secrecy that crime of every kind will become electronic and will take place in an instant once the decision is made. Drug operations, fraud, embezzlement, prostitution, blackmail, government conspiracies, military coups, murder. Much is possible now, but it can get worse. In the matter of terrorism, for example.

And even in business or education or government work, face-to-face meetings may no longer occur, and I think much will be lost there. It is really a sword with a double edge. Email. The Internet—an Information Super-highway, but one that is filled with—what are they called? Potholes?

It is the secrecy that is my worry. Split second. Cheap. Yes, cyberspace is good but can become evil. I am afraid this hemisphere and perhaps the whole planet has an analog intelligence dealing with a digital threat. That is how I see it.

Now back to cybernetics. It is a science that deals with how humans and machines can be similar and how controls can work in both. That is basically what my book is about.

(David) Would you mind explaining that again?

(Saltanban) Controls or feedback. I believe that eventually we can build a machine to imitate human behavior but, until that time, we should concentrate on controlling that behavior.

(David) What's the title of your book?

(Saltanban) *Mechanization: The Alternative to Cloning.*

(David) It sounds very ambitious.

(Saltanban) Not really. My premise is that machines should be able to accomplish more than the simple mechanization of work. After all, it is humans who are designing the machines.

(David) And?

(Saltanban) And through feedback or control, the machines can become more human. I have chapters in there on institutional conditioning, on biofeedback in medicine and even on transcendental meditation.

(David) *There*. Now we're talking.

(Saltanban) Now we are talking?

(David) Yes, that's what I'm interested in. Transcendental meditation. TM. In my medical field, there're so many patients say, with chronic infection who also have high blood pressure or asthma or migraines. If we could only teach them how to deal more effectively with their autonomic functions.

I know there are centers for this sort of thing—stress reduction techniques and the like—and they usually do a good job. But not always. Do you think it can be improved upon?

(Saltanban) Yes, of course.

> (David) Could you come and speak to our state medical society one of these days?
>
> (Saltanban) It would be my pleasure. If I could help someone, I would be honored.

The silence that ensued lasted longer than their hard, pinched facial expressions.

"End of CD," David said, relieved.

"I feel like I've gone through a ringer," Sparky complained.

"Not quite for me because I've listened to the tape several times now. What's your feeling about his cybernetics knowledge?"

"Knows his stuff, that's for sure. But on the subject of his book …about what machines should be able to do? Way out, I'm afraid."

Just as David slipped on his jacket and was about to leave, Chief Nick Medicore popped in.

"I heard you were here," he said, "so I thought I'd come over and say hello. I understand you've taken on the Radford case. You're not afraid of the position that puts you in?"

David's body tensed as he tried to hold back a smug expression. "I'm used to those positions," he said. "You want a more detailed answer?"

"Not really." The Chief's handshake was firmer than David could ever recollect.

"Well, I wish you luck. Call if I can help."

Medicore—sixtyish—was stocky, bald and pockmarked. He wore a light-colored turtleneck under a checked jacket and, as usual, kept his left hand in the side pocket of his trousers. David always felt it was to expose the gun holster clipped to his belt. And there was a badge somehow clipped to the holster.

The relatively warm reception took David by surprise, for it was uncharacteristic in a strained relationship dating back to when Medicore had arrived from the west coast. The Chief was openly dismissive at the start. And David reciprocated. So as their feelings thawed in due course, Kathy served as an intermediary, a kind of silent referee.

"Thanks a million," David smirked. "I'll keep that in mind."

Medicore edged closer to him and at his shoulder uttered, "If you want my opinion—for whatever it's worth—I don't approve of murders, but that guy certainly had it coming."

David decided to refrain from replying but his next thought came fast. *What's this: another unlikely comment from an unlikely source?*

The Chief turned to leave but not before giving David a thumbs-up and saying, "Remember. Let me know if I can help."

Alone with Sparky, David asked him if he had time to revisit the crime scene. "In fact, we could leave right now. I'll drive."

"Good. I'll make the time," the criminalist answered.

"I mainly want to vacuum the scene. Did anyone do it? It's been on my mind."

"Not that I remember. So few do nowadays, and I can't figure out why."

"Neither can I," David said. "After all the routine preliminary procedures, it completes the job. I can't understand why they leave it out. That's why they call it a vacuum *sweeper*—it sweeps up what might be left, what might have been overlooked."

Sparky gathered up his sleekly designed instrument from a closet and David watched as he attached two plastic pieces to its hose. He next mounted a metal screen on one of them to support a round piece of filter paper that would store the collected debris.

At the crime scene, they examined the governor's office, its anteroom and the balcony—inch by inch. Then David offered to do the sweeping, but Sparky took it upon himself to do so. He spent more than 20 minutes on the task and afterwards, when he detached the plastic pieces, he said, "Mostly hairs, fibers and dust particles."

"Wait a minute!" David exclaimed, "What are those?"

Stuck to the middle of the filter paper was a round piece of metal, tinier in diameter than the head of a one-inch nail. It was shaped like a small empty cup. And nearby was an ivory-colored bead, tinier than the cup. David wedged them out and carefully rotated them in the palm of his hand.

"See there on the inside surface of the …what? … cup, I guess?" he said. "It looks like dried adhesive. Be sure to save these, Spark. Put them in an envelope if you have to. Hold on to the filter and all the debris and, back at the lab, if the hairs and fibers don't match Radford's, let me know."

"Will do."

David put his arm around the criminalist. "Sorry," he said, "Didn't mean to give orders."

"They weren't orders. You were just consulting with me."

"Sure," David said with a laugh. "Do this, do that, do this. Consulting, that's all."

Walking slowly to his car, David felt unhinged. In fact it just occurred to him that he'd forgotten to stop by Kathy's office before they left headquarters. He was happy to have received Sparky's input thus far but—not even counting the Chief's closing words—after reading the manifesto and listening to the tape again, he had never anticipated what he was getting into.

What he'd thought was murder, pure and simple, had no doubt grown into something of international proportions. Or something even more sinister.

Chapter 5

As Kathy had predicted, Tilbud's Funeral Home was packed. Radford's wake was scheduled to begin at five, but she and David arrived at 4:15 and, on the way, he brought her up to date on what had occurred in Sparky's office. She too had read the manifesto and heard the CD before.

The weather had improved to a delightful spring afternoon, with a cyan blue sky and birds chirping in celebration. David wore an open collar yellow shirt and brown blazer, she a plain brown blouse and matching tight pants.

There was no space in the parking lot and the front and immediate side streets were filled with official looking cars and limousines. He recognized none as belonging to anyone he knew but they found a rare empty spot in a schoolyard five streets away and could identify none of the people scrambling by.

"All strange to me," she said as they mounted the raised walkway to the front entrance.

"Everything *about* the case is strange," he added, following on her heels.

The hundred feet or so to the door were jammed with people pressed against one another, all silent, grim-looking and slow moving. Every few seconds, they advanced as a unit, half a step at a time.

For want of something better to say, David leaned forward and whispered in her ear, "The outer surface of this building never changes, as if they replace the hardwood every year. Never fades."

Kathy remained silent.

A keystone was etched with *Tilbud* above the arched double door while a green awning spanned the entire walkway leading up to it. For some reason, the absence of front windows struck Kathy as appropriate, but she wondered aloud why an American flag she'd always noticed wedged into one of the voussoirs was no longer there.

David let it pass.

Once inside, the enormity of the plush and fragrant parlor allowed for the crowd with relative ease. They both signed the guest book, then moved about slowly, surveying everything and everyone in sight, yet after a full 10 minutes, still hadn't recognized anyone. They decided to skip the line that passed before an open casket and the one offering condolences to apparent family members.

"Where the heck *is* everybody?" Kathy asked David who was more interested in finding a rear or side entrance to take their leave.

"Like?" he said.

"Like people we know—forensic guys, the law, some hospital staff."

"Maybe it's just too early. Let's beat it anyway or once everyone arrives, we'll be here till nine."

"I'm game."

A tall, broad-shouldered man appeared from a side room off the main vestibule and marched directly toward David who instinctively eased his hand inside the left side of his jacket. The man looked vaguely familiar.

"Pardon me," the man said, "but are you Dr. David Brooks?"

David's hand reached the holster. "Yes, I am," he answered slowly.

"I didn't mean to startle you but I am Dr. Nadim Maloof."

David eyed him skeptically. "You mean from Egypt?"

"Yes indeed."

"The professor from Alexandria?"

"Yes again."

David's face brightened even as he said, "*The* Nadim Maloof?"

"Yes, I'm afraid so."

They shook hands and David introduced Kathy before asking, "How did you recognize me?"

"From photographs that Paul D'Arneau showed me when he came to one of my lectures at our university. We were both in the photos. That is, you and I. He talked about you quite a bit. All positive, I might add."

"Paul D'Arneau?" Kathy inquired, her eyes locked in David's direction.

"We were school chums, Kath, but I guess I never told you."

"Same kind of work. Right, doctor?" Nadim asked.

"Not quite. He looks for stolen treasures. I look for murderers. And do call me David."

"Is there any overlap …ah …David?"

"Sometimes."

"How so?"

"If there's murder and the stolen treasure is money. Like we have here."

Nadim appeared distressed.

"But my understanding is that no money was stolen, just discontinued. And by the way, in my spare time, I collect historical artifacts—not necessarily stolen but things of historical significance including furniture pieces, shards of pottery, archeological discoveries, military and police hardware. Even a small piece of

Dagobert's Throne from the Napoleon era. Things like that. And I pride myself in being an amateur historian of sorts. Once I started collecting the artifacts, I began delving into historical research."

"Quite a hobby," David said, then continued, "Paul told me about his trip there—in great detail actually. Very, very interesting. But tell me, what brings you here to a wake?"

"Juan Carlos Saltanban couldn't make it so he asked me to attend for him. Actually, I've killed two birds with one stone because I gave a lecture at Yale last night—on the preservation of historical artifacts."

David glanced at Kathy and felt his face harden. But with other things on his mind, he thought it imprudent to follow up on the subject.

"I'll be coming back to the area this Friday," Nadim said. "Another afternoon lecture at Yale. At its School of Management in conjunction with the medical school. This one will be on bio-engineering."

Again, David had no immediate interest in the man's lecture schedule.

"So you know Saltanban?" he asked suspiciously.

"I certainly do and he knows you. He told me he does. Quite a character, but a good business man."

"I'm sure." It was a forced response.

Nadim appeared to be about to deliver a speech he'd delivered many times and, as it turned out, he did.

"Let me explain," he began. "We met through our

association with crime figures, mainly those in Japan. As an aside, I'm aware of your interest in that country. Anyway, I know it sounds nefarious, but it really isn't. You see, I worked in Japan for eight years and became friendly with some well-known crime figures there, but I kept my distance. And I still do. I use them only as informants, and so does Juan. If you stop and think about it, the nature of their work makes them *reliable* informants. We all know they're involved with every kind of crime but at the same time—and I repeat—they're reliable."

David's new expression didn't waver, one of total absorption. And, deep down, he was hoping to hear more about Saltanban's current activities.

"If there isn't full reliability in dealings with others of their kind," Nadim continued, "they might be killed. Well, in return for information I receive from them, I help them with their health matters. Many of them are afraid to show up in doctors' offices or emergency rooms, so I make it easy for them. And the more friendly I became with the Japanese Yakuza, the more often I was put in contact with their counterparts all over the world: the Chinese Triads and Tongs, the Viet-Ching, the Sicilian and American Mafia. It's a unique arrangement, I know, but I have nothing to be ashamed of, as long as I don't participate in their racketeering. And . . ."

"Hold on a minute," David interjected. "You said that Saltanban also uses them as informants. You give them medical service, but what does he provide in return?"

"I'm really not sure. I think it's mostly because he and I are great friends and they all know it."

David didn't believe the last answer. "But why do you need informants?" he asked.

"It's helpful in our work. What I'm about to say might sound illegal, but it isn't at all. In fact the most successful entrepreneurs do the same thing."

Nadim paused as if to prepare a discreet way to express what was about to follow.

"The same thing? What's that?" David asked.

"Before meeting with prospective clients, we must know everything about them beforehand. The good and the bad."

"I see. That's sensible enough. Maybe meet with them casually at first—observing their body language. Very important. And I take it that you and Saltanban work together?"

"Yes, I work out of Alexandria, nearby Cairo and as far south as Aswan. And he works out of …just about anywhere. I've worked with him for some time now and we're really immersed in each other's business interests. I suppose that's the best way to put it. I'm mainly into bio-engineering, as you might have guessed."

"You mean he's interested in *that* too?"

"In everything and everywhere. Even in mining precious stones. I don't know where he gets his energy."

“Wait now,” David said. “You play a role in his cybernetics and telecommunications interests?”

“To a degree, yes. We often travel together on behalf of those things.”

“And you’re successful for the most part?”

“Yes. Quite. It would be 100 percent if it weren’t for politicians. They’re all crooked to begin with or soon become that way in order to survive in the game.”

Kathy’s nod was barely perceptible.

David backed up a few feet while raising his hand in a “stop” position, explaining he wanted to think about what was said thus far. In reality, he was taken with Nadim’s appearance. Their encounter had developed so fast—taking David by surprise—that he merely wanted to digest more about him from a distance. What he had said and what he looked like.

David took out a small notebook and pretended to write in it.

“You don’t mind if I make a note or two, do you?” he asked. It was a ruse he’d often resorted to, allowing him time to collect his thoughts, to sneak a look at the one before him, possibly to calculate his own next move or next sentence.

Nadim was dressed in a tan jacket, brown tie and dark trousers, the legs of which draped over most of his tan moccasin shoes. His snappy moves were at odds with his large frame. He had a dark complexion, gray mustache and thinning hair.

But it was his smile that David judged could dominate a room: easy, full, genuine. He was inclined to trust the man but couldn't justify Nadim's relationship with a person who had been on the run so often in years past.

David was also inclined to bring up that subject but didn't want to ruin a request he was planning to make. He pocketed his notebook and stepped forward.

"The room you came out of," he said. "I noticed it was empty and still is. Can the three of us have a seat in there? I want to ask a favor of you."

"Why, of course."

David led the way into the room where they sat in a circle. He had no idea how it would go, but knew he had to be truthful before reaching the meat of his question.

"Juan and I have had our battles in the past but I won't bore you with them," he began. "They're water under the bridge anyway. From what I've heard about him in the past dozen years and from what you've said about him, he sounds like a changed man. But I have to see for myself. You think he'd be willing to meet with me? And if so, I'd like to bring along an associate. Musco Diller's his name."

Nadim's answer was immediate, as if it were lying in wait for such a question. "Yes, and I'll make sure of it personally."

"Good. Very good. And can you arrange it all as soon as possible?"

"Yes, but now I have my own question."

"No problem. Shoot."

"Why do you want to see him? And don't answer if it's about something confidential."

It seemed obvious to David that Nadim must have known about the theories preceding Radford's murder, but he, David, didn't want to begin a review of them.

He drummed up the most vague answer he could and said simply, "All sorts of stories swirling around regarding your associate as a kind of benefactor in exchange for some supplies and things. You know, of course, that I've agreed with the authorities to look into the details of all that."

Each man fixated on the other's eyes. Nadim also smiled. David didn't.

"The bottom line is that I want to learn as much as I can about any agreements made. Things like who else they might have included. And I'd like to get it straight from the horse's mouth, so to speak."

David was uncertain about the wisdom of adding his next comment but went ahead with it anyway.

"Don't get me wrong, Nadim. I'm not implying Juan had anything to do with the murder, but he can provide some important insights." To his own satisfaction, David justified his lie by choosing the word "implying". Not, for example, "accusing" or "charging." A thin justification, but in the world of criminal investigations, such a tactic was commonplace.

"I understand," Nadim said. "I'll contact him tonight. He'll want to know how things went here and I'll mention meeting you both and learning of your request. I'd be surprised if he didn't want to talk with you."

David asked for and was given Saltanban's private office number. He would later share it with Musco in case either of them got sidetracked somewhere in Gibraltar.

In such a short space of time, David had achieved two main objectives, both accidental from his standpoint: an apparent meeting with Saltanban, and a conversation with his associate.

But he wondered whether or not they were accidental from Nadim's standpoint.

Chapter 6

It wasn't until late Wednesday afternoon that David and Musco were scheduled to visit with Saltanban. Nadim had laid the groundwork, including booking the flight from JFK to the Gib Airport and making reservations at the Caleta Palace Hotel.

On the trip over, Musco commented: "Aren't we lucky we're two of the rare birds who can shake off jet lag so fast?"

"Yeah, but that's not what's bothering me right now."

"What is?"

"The law that prohibits the carrying of a gun during commercial flights. I feel nude without one."

They agreed on staying overnight and leaving

for home in the early morning. "Unless something unexpected develops," David said.

Musco Diller was an old friend and a senior partner in Hollings' Red Checker Cab Company. For years, he had assisted David in many criminal investigations, utilizing his expertise as a world-class safecracker and lock-picker.

He was a wiry African-American who always wore a black cap with a rainbow band and shiny visor. Several tickets sprouted from the band—the same ones, year after year. His arms and legs looked like pipe cleaners, constantly in motion, and he had one glass eye that was a perfect match for the real thing. He now lacked a grizzled mustache which he said had become too difficult to maintain.

At about noon, they checked in at the hotel which, according to Nadim, was a mere stone's throw from Saltanban's office on nearby Catalan Bay. In reality, the bay was a tiny village nestled on the eastern side of the Rock.

He explained that the area was first used by the Genoese who followed the British Fleet, repairing its ships as required. He said that descendants of these shipwrights still lived in the sleepy village, that they were big in stature and sported large bushy mustaches as a tribute to their ancestors.

Their first floor room was compact but clean and tidy with twin beds and a balcony that looked out over an expanse of water with no visible end site. Ships could be seen off in the distance.

They heaved their luggage onto the beds and, after both commented that the room was adequate for their purposes, David said, "You know, we haven't eaten for hours and I don't know about you, but I'm starved and too tired to go back out."

"I'm not that tired," Musco said. "I saw some small pubs and restaurants nearby. I'd be happy to get some takeouts. What are you in the mood for?"

"Anything that's edible. I'll leave it up to you."

Musco left while David relaxed into a chair and picked up a magazine. Leafing through it, he came across an article that caught his attention. He read it in its entirety because, after meeting with Saltanban, he was determined to tour the Rock of Gibraltar from bottom to top, all 1400 feet, witnessing some of the interior areas described in the article.

St. Michael's Cave

St. Michael's Cave is thought to have attracted visitors since Roman times although prehistoric Neolithic inhabitants are known to have lived there much earlier. Within, the Cathedral Cave was long believed to be bottomless, probably giving birth to the story that Gibraltar was linked to Africa by a subterranean passage over 15 miles long under the Strait of Gibraltar.

The cave consists of an Upper Hall, with five connecting passages and drops between 40 feet and 150 feet to a smaller hall. Beyond this, a series of narrow holes leads to a further succession of chambers, reaching depths of some 250 feet below the entrance.

During World War II, the cave was prepared as an emergency hospital, but it was never used. While blasting an alternative entrance to the cave, a further series of deeply descending chambers ending in a small lake was discovered and named Lower St. Michael's Cave.

The Cathedral Cave is open to visitors and is an ideal auditorium for concerts, ballet, drama and presentations. The unique beauty of crystallized nature can be appreciated through a centuries-old stalagmite that became too heavy and fell on its side at the far end of the chamber.

David heard a knock on the door and suspected Musco had too much food in his hands to open it himself. He rose and opened it.

Four men, all tall, brawny and overly mustached, pushed David aside and burst into the room. Three of them kept their hands in their jacket pockets. The fourth identified himself as Tony and spoke fluent English.

"Now, don't say a word or make a silly move," he barked, "and you won't get hurt. Just come with us. Again, no questions asked."

David's first inclination was, indeed, to ask a question or two. Maybe they had come to the wrong room.

He felt his heart churning and tried to see if Musco was behind them. Unsuccessful, he took a chance with a single word.

"None?" he asked meekly.

"None. Just walk along with us to our van. We're driving up the Rock to a place I'm sure you've never seen. We'll keep you there until we receive further instructions. It might take awhile."

David felt fortunate he wasn't hammered by one of them for asking the single word.

Two of them grabbed him, one on each side, and the five men, closely aligned, shuffled down the corridor toward a back exit.

It wasn't long before the van reached the Cathedral Cave which David had read about just 20 minutes before. A single taxi preceded them, followed by a line of others.

David was glad he wasn't blindfolded, but reasoned his captors didn't want to alert anyone to what was happening.

On the way, he gawked at the historic Barbary apes, wishing they were human enough to understand the situation and seek help.

When they reached the fallen stalagmite—which David had also just read about—the van pulled off to the side. The men waited for all the taxis to pass before exiting the van and ushering David through a rusty gate, concealed by the stalagmite. The captors remained outside as he stooped to enter, offering no resistance for fear of facing rougher handling. Tony then creaked the gate shut and David thought he heard an echoing, "We'll be in touch."

The men secured a lock that had been dangling loose on a chain looped at one end of the metal gate. David wished Musco were there. He would have eventually picked the lock with ease.

He next recalled one of Tony's statements—"It might take awhile"—because initially, though he believed Saltanban had ordered his imprisonment, the statement seemed to contradict that.

Who then?

Through the bars, David said, "Now that I'm locked up, may I go ahead and speak?"

"Be my guest," Tony replied.

"Have you ever been in here?" Already, he was planning an escape, based on his vast knowledge of worldwide caves and tunnels. He had explored many of them and had taken classes in speleology while in the

Naval Investigative Service.

"No," Tony said laughing, "but I hear it's cool and cozy."

The men disappeared.

Straining to maintain his balance on craggy footing, David turned in a circle without feeling threatened, no doubt because he recognized the enclosure as a kind of anteroom to a cave tunnel. Though none was in sight, he reinforced his confidence by reviewing his many days of "caving" which included the negotiation of pitches, squeezes and water. But that was long ago. He had stopped it all once he'd reached age 40, but prior to that, he had regularly undertaken it for the sheer enjoyment of the outdoor activity itself, as well as for original exploration, like mountaineering or diving.

He recalled the time when the term "spelunking" came into disrepute, initiated by those "cavers" who considered spelunkers as déclassé among experienced enthusiasts. He sided with the cavers, and for years had a bumper sticker that read: "Cavers rescue spelunkers."

The illumination was dim but surprisingly adequate, good enough to evaluate his surroundings. He was enveloped in a montage of giant crystals and rock formations, most of which he could identify: the obvious stalactites and stalagmites, helictites, cave pearls, and baconstrips formed from multiple dripstones and soda straws. He hadn't even moved two feet and what he could make out, despite his experience, looked like an alien world seen for the first time.

Time to explore. But first back to the gate. It was just behind him and he stumbled only once until he reached out to grab it and push on it with his entire upper body. But there was no give. He examined its bars and hinges and found them all solidly attached.

Turning, his eyes were drawn toward a higher landing, beyond the overhang of a jagged side precipice. He found a gnarled length of wood propped against it and used it to help claw his way slowly upward. Very slowly.

Twice, he stepped on a rocky projection that split off, but managed to grasp others to keep himself from falling. And, halfway up, where he judged he was at the point of no return, he wondered why he had begun the ascent in the first place. But it did look brighter ahead.

Once atop the landing, he discovered that it looked no different or brighter from where he'd started. If anything, it was dimmer, more like semi-darkness. And the air was chillier. Frigid. Out of breath and coughing, he fell to his knees—then leaned back hard against a large rock, clouds of dust and pearly debris accentuating his cough.

And it was there that he had a moment to review thoughts of his captors and captivity, of the murder and possibly a second one. *It might take awhile*. Would it be his?

He remembered earlier times when he'd

volunteered to search for missing mountain climbers and was introduced to a phenomenon he'd never forgotten: "paradoxical undressing". That extremely cold temperatures over prolonged periods of time—hypothermia—could lead to death. Strange death, or what was termed an environmental death. One where victims are found undressed. He'd been told that such individuals had experienced hallucinations and subjective feelings of warmth that occurred in the terminal stages of the process. In addition, their bodies were found in a protected location—under a bed, behind a couch, on a shelf, *behind a boulder*. The theory was that this behavior was due to a primitive brain stem reflex of burrowing, as can be seen in hibernating animals.

David shuddered. He even checked his arms and position to assure himself that he wasn't overly cold and in a protected position. Nor was he hallucinating. Thus relieved, he squinted straight ahead and was able to make out a sloping, boulder-strewn tunnel that began far off—perhaps a golfer's delight of 95 yards.

This time, he was convinced he could see a sliver of light. He pulled himself up and headed in that direction, brushing away spider webs and dodging what sounded like bats flying by. As he trudged over unsure footing, and still craving some food—a sure sign that his ordeal hadn't wiped his appetite away—he thought how favorable it was that Tony and his goons hadn't passed beyond the gate with him, for he might not have had the opportunity to climb the precipice, as perilous as it was.

The physical patterns of a whole host of caves crossed his mind: branchwork, angular network, anastomotic, spongework, ramiform. He knew that most were composed of carbonate rock, but even when he reached the start of the tunnel, he couldn't decide what he'd be traversing.

One thing was clear, however: he'd be dealing with a steady stream of water. Possibly with tributaries that would converge from the sides, feeding into the main current. How high the current would get suddenly became his main concern. He rolled up his pants to his knees.

Three-quarters along, he made out a gate ahead, similar to the one he'd entered before and prayed it wasn't locked.

Throughout the entire length of the tunnel, the water came no higher up than his ankles and, reaching its end, the gate opened easily.

First he checked for passersby, then entered a passageway to what appeared to be one of the main chambers within the Rock. A wooden plaque hung on the wall to his right. He stopped to read its red lettering:

Great Siege Tunnels

The labyrinth of tunnels inside the Rock, including the Great Siege Tunnels, is arguably the most impressive defense system devised by humans. In 1783, at the end of the Great Siege, the commander of

> the French and Spanish troops, the Duc de Crillon, on being shown the fortifications that had led to the defeat of his troops, commented, "These works are worthy of the Romans." It highlights the ingenuity of those men who against all odds, endured the onslaught of the advancing forces and were still able to devise such a unique defense system.

David pivoted around to give the tunnel's exit a sarcastic salute, then found himself among a group of tourists. He hailed a cab that delivered him to ground level and onto the hotel.

In their room, he and Musco embraced, both speechless at first. David was the first to speak, blurting out all he could remember about the past hour and a half.

"If the bastards only knew you're right at home among rocks," Musco said.

"For the most part, anyway. And you, Musc, what did you think and do?"

"I didn't know *what* to do exactly. At first I thought you'd gone down to the lobby, checking on …whatever …but then as the minutes dragged on, I really began to worry. So I called Saltanban …had no trouble getting through to him …and I asked if you were there."

"How did he sound?"

"Happy I called but not happy with the news."

"Did he say what to do?"

"He said if you didn't return within the next half hour, that I should let him know and he'd contact the police. He sounded sincere about the whole thing, David."

"Then what?"

"I figured it best to stay here in the room in case you tried to get in touch with me."

Musco turned guilt-ridden. "Oh," he said, "I should tell you that I ate half the meal I brought back. Didn't enjoy any of it. The rest's for you."

They had been standing opposite one another. David then sat clumsily in a leather rolled armchair, missing its middle by a substantial amount and cursing.

He began rubbing the base of his left hand, an area he termed his "decision scar". It was a practice he'd begun while a teenager and, despite Kathy's reprimands, one he often called upon. During that time, what had been a nearly invisible scar from a minor athletic injury had become raised and obvious.

"I don't know about you," he finally said to Musco, "but I'd vote to spend half the time I'd planned with Saltanban and get outa here. Tonight maybe. Why wait for tomorrow?"

"I'm with you," Musco replied.

Pleased, David showered, changed into fresh clothes and devoured the rest of the meal. He then phoned Saltanban and parroted what he'd described to Musco.

"Well, old friend," Saltanban responded evenly, "I am glad you survived that experience. No harm done?"

"No harm done."

"Excellent. Why not come right over and we can chat? You know where my office is?"

"Yes, I received good directions."

"No, wait! I will send one of my men over to accompany you."

"Okay with me. We're at the Caleta."

"Yes, I know."

David and Musco were let off in front of Saltanban's office complex on Catalan Bay, at the far end of linked buildings, their blue-gray exteriors faded in the late afternoon light. Outside, his office appeared ordinary enough but once they passed through two sets of ebony double doors, only the unexpected unfolded before them.

Their breathing deepened as they beheld an expanse of interconnecting rooms with open entryways, about 50 in all, each with seated personnel apparently deep in thought, none of whom bothering to look up.

A narrow corridor forked around from front to back, a distance David estimated to be nearly the length of a football field.

The contents of each room were identical: a beech-colored swivel chair with a waterfall seat edge and contoured backrest; teak cabinets and tables that held computers, printers and copying machines; a shredder as large as a kitchen stove; and instead of a desk, a long table with a thick glass top suspended above a powder-coated steel frame on eight cubic pillars.

Just inside they were met by a stunning busty woman whose hair was as raven as the ebony doors.

"I know you're here to see Mr. Saltanban," she said without emotion. "This way, please."

She ushered them into a nearby side room, opening its door without knocking. "Here they are, Juan," she said, and then left.

"Ah," Saltanban said, smiling and rising sharply from his desk to greet David. They shook hands and Saltanban circled his left arm around David, patting his back.

David felt almost assaulted—by a man who was once his number one enemy. But he didn't let on, rather formally introducing Musco as his co-worker in investigative affairs.

Musco initiated a handshake and identified himself as the one who had called before.

"Investigative affairs? Meaning I am being investigated?"

Still no contractions, David observed.

The man before him was as hefty as a bar bouncer and, as always, stuck out his chest as if to highlight two silver medals that dangled from the jacket of his double-breasted dark suit. His hair, still dense and curly, was solid black—ostentatiously dyed— in contrast to a goatee sprinkled with gray. And unlike before when he stood erect, he was now stooped. David also observed a fine hand tremor and a gaze that was more distant than focused.

"The short answer is no, which I'll get to in a minute," David said, "but first let me compliment you on your set-up here. Very, very impressive! And those shredders. I've never seen so many so big."

"Yes, they are all necessary. Much of what we do here is by trial and error."

David thought he understood what that meant, but wasn't totally sure.

"And you have quite an office. No shredder, I see."

"Yes again. By the time decisions get to me, I have very little to correct. My workers know how I think."

"Well, you have nearly everything you need, that's for sure." David's hands spanned the office.

"Yes, that is for sure."

The centerpiece of the office was a 15 baluster desk. David had made a point of counting them. Its top was a single thick slab of wood. On each end was a desktop world globe. Fluted column bookcases lined the walls. Four burlap-cushioned chairs were spread before the desk and on the wall behind it was a large map of Europe—maybe a reproduction of a centuries-old effort. There were no windows.

"Before we get to why I'm here," David said, still

looking around, even running his hand gently across the desk, "one simple question: what's all this furniture made of?"

"Solid elm reclaimed from a 19th century French courtyard," Saltanban answered proudly. He signaled for them to sit after arranging the chairs for easy discussion.

There was a palpable lull in their conversation before David returned to the reason for the visit.

"As I said, we're not here to investigate you, Juan. I just want to clarify some things first-hand." He didn't allow time for a response. "You're aware of course that Governor Radford was murdered."

"Indeed. That is so sad."

"That's the thing I want to clarify so it might help in the overall investigation."

All the while, David was hoping Juan would have said something that might be incriminating, but nothing materialized to that point.

David proceeded. "Prior to the murder, Radford suddenly and without warning discontinued funding for many projects and—let's call them—supplies. Many groups and organizations in Connecticut felt the brunt of it. And he even used his influence to curtail the same things beyond the state's borders. Now, you and your company—I should say companies—were the principle ones that were adversely affected, I take it?"

Juan remained silent as if he expected an elaboration.

He sank slightly in his chair and his face lost its distant look.

David felt he had to follow up immediately. "What I mean is that you …and others, to be sure …lost significant business."

Juan straightened to full sitting height.

"I am afraid that is true but knowing you, my friend, you must appreciate that I also do business elsewhere. So what I lost by Radford's action has already been made up in additional business around the world."

Simultaneously, he leaned over to spin one of the globes.

David had reached the pinnacle of his trip to Gibraltar but wanted more.

"Where are you concentrating now, or is that privileged information?"

"No, no, it is not privileged. In fact, the more people know about it, the more business can grow."

Juan stared at Musco who had begun taking notes. David noticed.

"You do not …I mean …you don't mind if Musco takes notes, do you?"

"No. That is fine. It makes me feel important."

What a crock, David thought.

"Anyway," Juan said, "you asked what has taken the place of my business in Connecticut. It is Argentina. Buenos Aires to be exact. A beautiful city. I have entered into a business I have never handled before. You will never guess what it is."

"I'm afraid not."

"Informants told me that many of their mausoleums were deteriorating on their outer surfaces, perhaps because of the many visitors touching them. Wear and tear, you know. Especially in what is called the Recoleta Cemetery. It contains row after row of elegant and elaborate commemorations to those who have passed on. They say each mausoleum competes with the next in style and scale. The result is an amazing collection of architectural masterpieces, associated with names that make up a 'Who is Who' of Argentine history-makers. People like Eva Perón."

David interrupted. "I don't understand. I mean I agree with you that it's a beautiful city. Kathy and I were there not too long ago. Stayed at the home of an old Navy buddy of mine, Joe Gomez. Funny, both of us went into law enforcement. Still exchange Christmas cards and an occasional letter. In fact he helped her put together the most complete scrapbook of the city. She does that for each of our travel journeys—ocean cruises, river cruises, long land trips and the like. I've referred to the one covering Buenos Aires several times. You remember Kathy, don't you?"

"Yes, I do. Nice lady and a very good police detective."

"Thank you, and pardon my ranting. But back to the tombs: yes, maybe the exterior surfaces of some of them are scuffed up. How do you fit in though?"

"I have contracted to replace them."

"Completely?"

"No, not necessarily. The outside and whatever is needed inside."

Earlier, upon hearing the word "informants," David had thought of Nadim Maloof.

"Interesting," David said. "By any chance …is Nadim Maloof involved in any of this new venture?"

"He certainly is. He is what I would refer to as my point man over there."

"I see. But getting back to Radford. He worked for you for some time right here, didn't he?"

"Yes he did, but not for long. Maybe a year or two. He held a minor position in our medical cybernetics division."

"And you got along?"

"Yes. We hardly came in contact with each other, but he did his job well." Juan raised an eyebrow and added, "I cannot believe he would eventually become a governor."

Still harboring past resentments, David couldn't resist: "You must be aware of the many entanglements of politics: strange bedfellows and all that?"

"I feel the same way."

David was about to bring up the subject of his captivity and was surprised when Juan brought it up himself.

"Your hell in a cave," Juan said, "That must have been a scary time. Who would want to do such a thing …and why?"

David smiled guardedly. "Beats me," he said. "But as long as you brought it up, I'd just as soon leave for home tonight rather than tomorrow. Possible?"

"I do not blame you. There is a flight to JFK that leaves here at seven." Juan checked his watch. "I use it all the time."

David's thoughts were primarily on getting back to the States safely. And he had heard enough to justify the trip. Nonetheless, after also checking his watch, he said, "We'd better hustle, but may I ask you two personal questions?"

"Yes, go right ahead."

"Why did you settle here in Gibraltar?"

"Favorable taxation." David saw that Musco was still taking notes.

"And lastly, you know Alton Foster, our administrator at Hollings?"

"Yes. Very well. We have lunch whenever I visit Connecticut."

"You say it as if you'll be visiting there again."

"I hope so."

David decided to take a chance. "May I ask if he was ever on your payroll—or is that out of bounds?"

"Not out of bounds. The answer is yes. But not on a payroll. Just a gift of appreciation."

"Monetary?"

"Monetary."

David didn't have the nerve to ask the amount but did inquire if the gift was given on a regular basis.

Juan answered in the affirmative.

David was about to check his watch, but remembered he already had. He and Musco rose and after thanking Juan profusely—Musco more sincerely than David—they took their leave.

On the flight home, David puzzled over how a man with an imaginary son could create such a large business empire.

PART TWO:
THE TRAVELER

Chapter 7

On Thursday afternoon, Connecticut time, David popped in to see Kathy who was seated at her office desk. Startled, she screamed, "David! You're back so soon?"

He ran his hands down both sides of his face and replied, "I *think* it's me."

Kathy overlooked the intended humor and said, "But I thought …I mean . . ."

Before she could complete the sentence, he described what he labeled a Gibraltar adventure, leaving out many of the details regarding the cave and tunnel, yet indicating he and Musco had left earlier than planned in order to avoid anything worse.

"You weren't hurt, were you?" she asked.

"No, just a few scrapes and bruises. Nothing serious."

"Thank God! But was it worth it to travel that far to meet with Saltanban?"

"Okay for starters."

She got up, walked past her desk and threw her arms around him. He reached down and as they embraced, their lips met as if it were one of their first kisses.

"Oh, David," she said, "I don't know about this. Those black SUVs, the warning note and now caves and tunnels. I just don't know."

"It'll be fine, Kath, once I get a handle on it all." He backed away and crossed his arms in a defensive pose. "Only problem is, I'm not totally sure how or where to continue."

Kathy didn't hesitate. "Interviews, interviews, interviews. You've told me that a million times. 'It's the backbone of interrogation' you'd say. 'In fact an interview is an interrogation'." She had deepened her voice to mimic him.

"I suppose that's right," he responded distantly. "And how better than to check with the hospital people? I'll start at the top."

"Foster?"

"Our good old administrator, Alton Foster. Reminds me: I left something out before. Saltanban said that Foster was on the take. For some time."

"On the take from whom?"

"From him: Saltanban."

"Did he say why?"

"I didn't quiz him on it. I just assumed it was because Foster steered so much business his way."

Kathy returned to her chair.

"You know what?" she asked, not waiting for an answer. "It's been so long since you spent a decent amount of time at the hospital. Think about it: Friday morning grand rounds when not on your out-of-town cases; once-a-month Board meetings—again, when available. And that's about it. For 12 years. You practically lived in the place before that."

"I agree," David said, "but what does that get me? I mean spending time there."

"Who knows? Mosey around, have lunch with some of the docs in the cafeteria, see some of your old buddies in Radiology. You might pick up the latest gossip, even some good leads. Things you might not have learned otherwise."

He stomped one foot with a flourish and said loudly, "That's it. *That's* what I'll do!"

"You're making fun of me," Kathy said.

"I'm kidding, of course. You're absolutely right. I knew what it would get me all along. I just wanted to see if you agree."

She shot him a scorching look. "Sometimes you're hopeless," she said.

Her secretary appeared at the door and said

hurriedly, "There's a person-to-person phone call from Argentina!"

"Argentina?" Kathy asked. "For me?"

"No, for David."

"What the . . ." David said and picked up the phone. "Yes? David here."

"David Brooks?"

"Yes."

"Hello, sir. I am Cristina De la Fuente calling from Buenos Aires." Even the pronunciation of her name sounded anguished. "I hope I'm not bothering you but . . ."

"Wait please," David said. "How do you know of me but, more important, how did you know I was here?"

"Nadim Maloof mentioned you and your friend … Kathy is it?"

"That's correct. She's my fiancée. But may I ask: you were born in Argentina?"

"Yes. Buenos Aires."

"Your English is remarkably good."

"Thank you. I lived in New York for most of my early life."

David brought her attention back to Nadim and she elaborated.

"He told me about your investigative work and where you live and your phone number and said that Kathy worked in your police department. I tried your house and there was no answer, so I took a chance you might be there with her."

David signaled Kathy to pick up a second phone on a nearby counter.

"Okay. And the purpose of your call?" David asked.

"He said that if I was ever . . . ever . . . called by you, not to give away any information about our agreements."

"What agreements?"

"He, that is Nadim, works for and I suppose is paid by a Mr. Saltanban to improve some of our precious properties . . .our mausoleums. But, Mr. Brooks, Nadim is demanding money directly from our government plus many of Eva Perón's artifacts. He said he has a miniature museum just off his office in the Faculty of Medicine Building in Alexandria. He stressed he wanted the artifacts even more than the extra money. He sounded frantic about it"

"*The* Eva Perón?"

"Yes. Evita. Some of her gowns, photographs, suits, dresses, jewelry—and many, many other things that belonged to her or were associated with her.

"For example, she was always accompanied by the same two soldiers—for protection. You know of course that she died in her early thirties. Cervical cancer. And in her declining weeks, when travel was no longer possible, the two men gave many of their military accessories to the Perón family. Like epaulets, wrist bracelets, badges, medals, cuff links, caps adorned with her picture, pistols in their holsters still attached to the belts they wore, even boots with protective knives in their sockets. They look more like daggers. They gave all of these things in pairs. Which was really generous of them because they're probably worth a fortune now. Anyway, the family eventually donated them to the museum here in Buenos Aires, the Museo Evita." The woman had spoken rapidly, as if reading from a text.

"But getting back to that Nadim fellow," she continued, "I'm the leader of a committee to work with him and was told he was getting paid by Mr. Saltanban. I asked Nadim about it when he was here yesterday and he said it wasn't enough. I tried to talk him out of it, but he said he would go directly to our highest government leaders to ask for more. He said he was being cheated and if he didn't receive what he deserved, that the work would come out …what is it? I wrote the word down. *Shabby*."

"So it's artifacts and additional money that he wants."

"Yes."

"Is he still there?"

"No, he only stayed one day."

They exchanged what would ordinarily be considered pleasantries but David's mind was ticking too fast to appreciate them. Or to ask about anything more, such as the status of the restorations, the amount of demanded money, and whether or not Nadim had already spoken to high-level authorities. And if he could believe what he had just heard, he entertained a hunch, one that pertained to a possible rift between Saltanban and Nadim. Perhaps they couldn't agree on Nadim's worth.

He thanked Cristina for the call and took down her phone number, after saying he would look into the situation. He hung up the phone delicately. As did Kathy.

"Well I'll be!" David said. "What the hell is going on?"

"Who knows, except the plot thickens. I think you'd better call Nadim or, better still, Saltanban."

"I think Saltanban." He checked the clock on the wall. "But it's sorta late over there now and besides, it can wait till tomorrow. I've had enough for one day. Let's go home and relax."

"If we can."

"First thing there …besides pouring drinks … is reviewing your scrapbook on Buenos Aires. Maybe there's something you covered that might be of value. And when I talk with Saltanban, I'm asking what amount of money this is costing Argentina and what's Nadim's take. I'm tired of not probing the way I should."

Home before six, they indeed had their white wine, he two glasses, she one. They showered together and then, not in a talkative mood, he swept into their study and searched the titles of the two or three dozen scrapbooks lined up in a pair of bookcases. Kathy followed him. He selected the thickest, one marked “South America”. Half the book was devoted to Argentina and half of that to Buenos Aires.

He flipped through the pages and skimmed through selected entries that Kathy had made—doting on each sentence:

> Buenos Aires is a huge and busy port. Mammoth machinery at dock to move immense containers. Some stops on tour bus. One to the Recoleta Cemetery. Amazing maze of mausoleums. Evita’s body there. Also to Plaza de Mayo and Casa Rosa where she spoke from balcony. According to our guide she was loved by the poor, but hated by the rest. Symbols on pavement for bodies of soldiers. Few more stops, then to Claridge Hotel where we stayed.
>
> Another section of town that stimulates the senses is La Boca, at mouth of Rio Plata. A former warehouse district, this section of B.A. is a bit funky, decorated with brightly painted, tin-roofed wooden houses that serve in dual role: as backdrops for local painters working on, exhibiting and selling their work and

as colorful backgrounds in the paintings themselves.

Next day took cab to Dorrengo Square in San Telmo district for delightful time. White statue/mimes, musicians, tango dancers—all in the midst of a flea market. There, among plenty of pricey junk, are antique treasures, many made and purchased in Europe before the 1940s.

Still another architectural masterpiece linked to history is the awesome Teatro Colon where, for instance, Maria Callas and Enrico Caruso appeared repeatedly. Outstanding acoustically and famous for opera, it is also an architectural incongruity. The building is Italianate, but the décor is French. The auditorium imitates a scintillating wedding cake, done in red velvet.

We read a circular that said it all: "In a compliment to both cities, Buenos Aires is frequently dubbed the Paris of South America. The comparison stems from the decidedly European flair found in the food, the cafes and the chic boutiques. It shines

> out of the city's noble architectural beauty and sings from its sophisticated cultural attractions. Yet look deep into this highly polished veneer and you will find that Buenos Aires—like its signature dance, the tango—has a wild Latin passion bubbling just below its stately surface."

The only parts David reread were those referring to the Recoleta Cemetery, paintings in La Boca, and antique treasures made in Europe. He dwelled on each for an extended period of time but in the end was reasonably convinced that nothing Kathy had entered in the scrapbook was of value in his latest investigative role.

As they readied for bed, the phone rang. It was Sparky calling.

"Sorry to bother you so late," he said, "but I, myself, just got a call from a wood expert friend of mine and, rather than waiting till morning, I figured it was important enough to phone you about it tonight."

"No bother at all. What's up?"

"The wooden handle of the dagger?"

"Yeah . . ."

"It came from Argentina. He even narrowed it to Buenos Aires."

David, instantly dazed, could barely make out Kathy at the dressing table. "It's Sparky. The dagger's handle came from Buenos Aires," he shouted.

It took more than several moments to collect himself before apologizing to Sparky for his reaction. “The point, Spark, is that so many things are linking that city to this crime. It can’t just be happenstance.”

Chapter 8

David decided to attend Friday morning's medical Grand Rounds, but not before phoning Juan Saltanban in Gibraltar. The call went through quickly, and almost as quickly Juan asked if there was a problem.

"In a way," David replied. He had already deemed it unnecessary to call attention to Sparky's news.

"Right after getting home yesterday," he said, "I received a call from a woman in Buenos Aires." He checked a scrap of paper. "Name is Cristina De la Fuente. She says that Nadim Maloof is demanding extra money and artifacts …Eva Perón artifacts …from Argentine officials because of the work he's supposedly supervising there. She and others I assume, are furious. Says she's the head of a group overseeing it all. You have any idea what this is about? Isn't he working for *you* and isn't he on salary?"

Juan didn't respond immediately but finally said, "This is news to me. I mean what he is demanding. I would doubt he would do so. It would be behind my back and he is not that kind of man. As for payroll—yes, he is on a pro rata basis."

"May I ask what he's getting for this project?"

"You may ask but I am afraid I cannot give you an answer. If he wants to share that with you, it is his business."

David detected a degree of umbrage, yet followed with, "Then can you tell me—since you're the ultimate …the ultimate boss, I would call you …can you tell me what the overall cost is to Argentina?" He felt his own umbrage taking hold.

"No, because that would violate the rules. If Argentina wants to tell you, just like with Nadim, that is their business."

"What rules?"

"What?" Juan sounded perturbed.

"You said 'rules'. What rules?"

"Business rules," Juan said, and hung up.

David sat at his desk fuming but after reconciling the hostility he may have created and, as a result, calming down, decided to call Nadim. And, because he hadn't gotten a chance to discuss the Evita artifacts with Juan, he spent more time on that subject than on the financial issue. Nadim unflappably denied everything Cristina had alleged.

David approached Kathy who was applying the last of her makeup. He described the phone calls.

Her response was, "Let it be."

After she was ready for work and he had completed some pacing, he joined her at the kitchen table for a second cup of coffee.

"This isn't going to upset your day of interviews, is it? At the hospital, right?" Kathy reached over to cup her hands over his.

"Right," he said. He reminded her he would only interview those who had openly favored the hospital's transition to both a clinical and research institution, not those who opposed it.

He expanded on some details, concluding with his opinion that only those who had favored the transition would have felt betrayed by Radford. That since he had cut off the necessary funding, the whole changeover would eventually be in jeopardy.

"So you'll interview very few," she said.

"Only two right now: Alton Foster and Phil Bennett, the psychiatrist." David then waved off any more hospital questions with a peremptory gesture.

"I still call Saltanban a son-of-a-bitch," he said.

"The importance of those answers isn't . . ."

"Wait up," David said, his voice a notch higher than before. "It isn't the answers, it's who's telling the truth?

Cristina or that manipulator?"

Kathy peered down her nose. "Isn't that a pretty strong word, my dear?"

"Maybe so. We'll wait and see."

David always admired the hospital which was crammed into Hollings' eastern hillside. Not so much the administrative section or the various wings or the most recent addition, but its commanding clock tower, a century-old structure that had required little maintenance throughout its life span. It featured square clocks on all four sides and was shaded by a copper cupola. The red brick tower still reminded him of a foundation pile in reverse as he descended the steep hill toward the doctors' parking lot.

He deliberately arrived early so he could exchange opinions about the murder with the two staff members he'd cited with Kathy. And possibly others. Alton Foster would be the first. Technically he wasn't on the medical staff, but was interested in and attended many of its meetings.

It was a holdover interest from two years of surgical training at a renowned medical center. He had been dismissed for publicly unspecified reasons. But privately, he complained about the rigors of the program, especially the night hours.

David spotted the administrator alone at a corner table in the cafeteria and headed his way, half cup of coffee in hand.

Elongated planters separated rows of tables around them, an architectural design that deadened conversations. David thought it a perfect setting for the questions he had in store.

They hadn't seen each other in weeks but shook hands and said their hellos as if it had been years. Once seated, David didn't waste any time.

"I met with Juan Saltanban," he began.

"Saltanban? How is the old geezer?"

"Geezer, schmeezer—he's worth millions."

"Tell me about it."

"He said he gave you plenty." David exaggerated on purpose.

"I wouldn't say plenty but, yes, he gave me reimbursements." As he spoke, Foster removed his glasses and cleaned its lens with a tissue.

"Reimbursements for what?"

"For supplying him with leads."

"Leads leading to money, right?"

"That's cute, doctor, but hardly appropriate. Look, he did a lot for people like us."

"Us?"

"Yes. My administrator friends at other hospitals, nursing homes and independent clinics. And he brought us up to snuff on the latest technologies."

"For a price."

"Of course for a price."

"Was it a decent price?"

"Okay, but nothing to write home about."

"Steadily?"

"What's that supposed to mean?"

"Like a regular salary?"

"Regular enough."

"Were those others happy with the arrangement?"

Foster looked flustered. "How should I know? We never discussed it. And why are you questioning me like this?"

David didn't want to press too hard—to reach the point he had with Saltanban. "Sorry," he said, "just getting background stuff, that's all."

It was his version of an apology, but Foster didn't take it that way.

"Well if you're insinuating I had a close tie with him, you're mistaken."

David stirred his cup although there was no coffee left in it.

"You know me better than that, Alton. I don't insinuate. Regardless though, let's switch the subject. What did you think about Radford's murder?"

"Think? Terrible, but with more enemies than friends, he had it coming from what I can tell. His action certainly didn't help *us* any."

"You mean canceling the funding?"

"Precisely."

"Did you like him?"

"I didn't know him ...never met him. Never wanted to."

After a few run-of-the-mill questions and answers, they left the cafeteria for Grand Rounds, Foster taking shortcuts, David sauntering along the longer route, hoping to meet up with other doctors. He didn't. At least none he knew. There had been such a changeover since his more active days at Hollings that he simply returned the smiles of the many he passed who had stethoscopes draped over their shoulders. But he did exchange a few words with some older nurses, unit clerks and orderlies. One orderly indicated they were now called medical techs.

Rounds were held in the Tanarkle Room. Renamed after Dr. Ted Tanarkle, the chief pathologist who was one of the murder victims 12 years before, it was a good-sized room with walls lined with photographs of past Chiefs of Staff, David among them. There were about 40 rows of chairs before an elevated stage with podium, white screen and the usual equipment needed for power-point presentations. The room was half-full when David arrived at 8:50.

He happened to sit next to Dr. Philip Bennett, the relatively new head of the psychiatry department. Bennett had replaced Dr. Samuel Corliss who was three years retired.

"Phil, how *are* you?" David said. Their handshake was prolonged.

"I'm fine but haven't seen you in ages, David.

Where you been keeping yourself?"

"Me keeping myself? It's the cases that've been keeping me."

"Full-time on the Radford one, no doubt."

"No doubt. Listen, you're a psychiatrist. What do you make of it?"

Bennett straightened his tie and said, "I don't think it takes a psychiatrist's mind to decipher this one."

David stared at him pensively. "You mean you know who the killer is?"

"No. I mean there are plenty of killer candidates out there who probably had reason to do the job. Across the entire state and even in others."

David didn't comment, expecting a tag to Bennett's remarks.

The psychiatrist went on. "May I use a non-professional word to define his behavior, both in the business world and politically?"

"Of course."

"He *screwed* everybody in one way or another. To seal business contracts, to advance in politics. The only difference in politics, as you well know, David, is not to screw more than 50 percent of other politicians. He apparently didn't, and that's why he got elected. What a system!"

"Hmm, not bad for a psychiatrist," David said.

Bennett ignored the dig, instead saying: "Maybe we could talk further about this and some other things

I have on my mind. You've been around for some time and I'd like your opinion. I'm through with patients early on Fridays. How about stopping by my office today … say at about one o'clock?"

David thought such a visit had reciprocal value and accepted the invitation.

In addition to little familiarity with most staff physicians, he had trouble visualizing the Hole, a place he called his office at one time, not where he saw patients but where many of their records were stored.

It was previously a storage room with flaking walls and ceiling. Where many had banged heads on low-hanging pipes that snaked around here and there. Where one could easily smell medicinal and detergent crosscurrents from the pharmacy and laundry room on opposite ends of the corridor and daily caravans of laundry carts nearly knocked people off their feet. He had willfully kept away from that basement floor when attending the many Grand Rounds and Board meetings since his retirement from active practice. The excuse he gave to those who asked why he shunned his old stomping grounds was always the same: "It's a matter of nostalgia, sentiment," and he would let it go at that.

Belle, his longtime secretary, and Virginia Baldwin, the nursing supervisor and once his principal confidante, were both still working in the hospital and often tried to schedule a "reunion party" there but he never gave in. Even Kathy couldn't succeed.

But this time was different, and after hearing about a litany of boring cases during an hour of Grand Rounds, he decided to visit the Hole for one specific purpose: to meditate. In the past he would frequently lock the door and sit in a special swivel chair to dwell on difficult medical cases, to let problems and possibilities percolate. To be alone with them, isolated from outside distractions, seated in his "magical" chair. It would clear his mind from everything other than the cases or anything else troubling him. He could have meditated the same way at home but for some unexplainable reason, it never worked there. He had tried but had never gotten very far. Maybe, he once thought, it had something to do with his unusual surroundings in the Hole. An "important" hospital person assigned to an unimportant room, one he described as ratty. And to offset the incongruity, he could think harder and harder—deeper and deeper. It was almost like a séance. A private séance for one person.

He wanted now to accomplish the same thing, for he had encountered situations and changed personalities in too short a time and his mind was in turmoil.

He entered the room cautiously, switched on the twin overhead lights and was disturbed by what he saw: a collection of broken I.V. poles, bed stands, old stretchers and stack after stack of bedpans. The ugly lines of the Hole held no sanctuary now as he had once thought. But in the midst of it all, partially hidden under two overturned tables, was the swivel chair!

He yanked it free, wiped off a layer of dust and sat on it, gingerly turning from side to side and leaning back. There was no resistance, no squeaking. He felt right at home, the one where he had often mulled over lab results and had narrowed diagnostic possibilities. This time he envisioned a list of things that had plagued him since he agreed to take on the investigation. He even numbered them:

1. Details of the murder, including the strange dagger.
2. My eagerness to return to the murder scene to conduct my own forensic evaluation.
3. My preliminary suspect list.
4. Cristina De la Fuente's claim involving Nadim's demands.
5. The very reference to Eva Perón.
6. The black SUV. Who drove it?
7. The note attached to the wiper blade. Who placed it there?
8. My captivity in the cave and tunnel. Who ordered it?
9. Saltanban's changed behavior and his monetary empire.
10. Disturbing comments by Alton Foster, Bruno Bateman and even Chief Medicore.

David felt he missed an issue or two, but after a

half hour in the chair, he had reached some conclusions. More like admonitions, really: stop being hounded, wondering about the tiniest of details so early in the case. Stop dithering and get on with the interrogations. All ten issues, taken as a whole can easily “hound”, but each individually should not. Consider most of them as past tense and deal with the present and future.

He regarded the minutes in the Hole as worth it, but wasn’t certain he’d return there again. And he was unable to fathom why not.

He hadn’t forgotten his one o’clock meeting with Dr. Bennett, but that was at least three hours away. He would look up Belle who had become a unit clerk on the eighth floor’s orthopedic department, and after lunch, perhaps visit with Virginia Baldwin in the nurse’s wing.

Because of David’s full schedule, he’d never arrived for Board meetings early nor remained behind afterwards, so he never had a chance to meet with either of them for several years.

He took an empty elevator to the eighth floor where he found Belle sorting out folders at a desk within the nurses’station.

“David!” she cried out and quickly covered her mouth. Doctors’ and nurses’ heads turned.

“Belle, you never change.” He pulled over a chair as if he’d intended to stay for some time.

“In appearance or disposition?” she asked. She was in her late thirties, blonde, diminutive and shapely.

"Both. That is, if your disposition's the same as when you worked for me."

"Was it good or bad?"

"Good, or I wouldn't have put it that way."

"David, you haven't changed either," she said softly, rising to kiss him on the cheek. There never was a "thing" between them 12 to 15 years before.

"I see you've taken over the Radford case," she said.

"Yeah. You have anything helpful to say about it? Any scuttlebutt around here?"

"Don't know if it's helpful but it's become **the** conversation. Even at the Sheraton the other night. We had our annual Auxiliary Dinner and Mr. Foster got up to give his speech and started off indirectly saying that we should knock off talking about the murder so much."

"What do you think about him?"

"No comment."

They reminisced about the old days, David even admitting he missed caring for patients. Then he left for an early lunch at the cafeteria.

Afterward, he looked for Virginia Baldwin at her office but was told she had a cold and had taken the day off.

David was early for his appointment with Dr. Bennett, but decided it was just as convenient to sit in his waiting room as it was to sit elsewhere or to roam the floors aimlessly.

The doctor opened his private office door at one on the button. “Aha, you’re here,” he said. “Come in; come right in.”

Inside, the office appeared the same as when Bennett’s predecessor occupied it: basic leather couch, two recliners, maple desk and high-back chair. Its ivory side walls were still sprinkled with diplomas, certificates and photographs of class reunions. Paintings of Sigmund Freud and Karl Menninger dominated the wall behind the desk.

The psychiatrist, a fellow Board member, was in his late forties, about six-feet tall and impressively trim. He wore a well-tailored blue suit and was known to sport brightly colored vests. This time it was red. His dark hair, combed straight back, was gray at the temples and his smooth face was flushed. It gave David the impression that his collar was too tight and he told him so.

Bennett laughed and said, “You’re not the first to say that. But, no, I’ve always had a red tinge. At least that’s what my mother told me.”

David felt playful. “There you go, Phil, just like the other guys in your field. Explaining everything by reverting back to childhood.”

“You may have a point, but things have changed some.” Bennett’s eyes took on a wounded look. “And speaking of change, that’s why I wanted to see you.”

He pointed to one of the chairs. “Please sit,” he said.

"Thanks." David eased the chair closer to the desk. "But I can't stay long, Phil. I have a ton of things to do."

Bennett looked around the room as if checking for eavesdroppers, then said, "I want your opinion. I'm thinking of changing my kind of practice. Frankly, I'm tired of people's mental problems. There's more to medicine than that."

His comments were short and crisp—statements, not sentences.

"And becoming what?" David asked.

"Maybe a hospitalist. I had some training in E.R. work early on."

"And in psychiatric research, I'm told."

"Yes but I'm tired of that, too."

David wanted to learn more before offering an opinion. "Not being hasty, are you?" he inquired.

"Not at all. Wife's all for it. I think a two-year fellowship would do it."

"Where?"

"Don't know yet."

"'Yet' means you've made up your mind."

"I'd say that. Maybe I should throw in the word 'practically'."

"When?"

"Not sure."

"Told anyone else here?" David had begun to imitate the cadence.

"No."

"You want my opinion?"

"Yes. I'd welcome it."

"Go for it. You sound sincere and I agree there's more to medicine than exploring how a person thinks. Being a hospitalist would give you a great variety of challenges. Basically in several fields all at once."

David interpreted Bennett's gracious smile as bringing the subject to an end. It was confirmed when the psychiatrist reached over for a handshake.

"Now then," David said. "I'd like your opinion on two or three things."

"I'm all ears."

"What's your take on Governor Radford's murder?"

"Like who might have done it?"

"Yes."

"I'd go with the consensus. He—or she, for that matter—could have come from a whole host of people because he wasn't very well liked."

"Did you care for him?"

"Can't say I did—based on what I'd heard."

"Most can't understand how he got elected."

"Put me in with that group, David. But you know politics as well as anybody else."

"Don't get me going on politics, pal. You'd be late for dinner. But one last thing because I must leave. How do you feel about the new arrangement here? About becoming primarily a research center?"

"Well, as you know from our Board meetings, I always favored it. But now, if I follow through and end up elsewhere, I suppose I'd be lukewarm on it. Anyway, the funding's been stopped and I don't know how long Hollings can continue this way. I'd call it a mess. A mess in limbo."

Before leaving, David said, "Good luck, Phil. And if you need a letter of recommendation, you can count on me."

Chapter 9

It was a little past one-thirty. David spent the next hour or so interviewing Bruno Bateman at the martial arts studio and Chief Medicore at police headquarters. In both instances, they spent more time talking shop than on what David had come for in the first place. He deliberately wanted it that way so as to take the pressure off the questions that would eventually follow.

When that time came, he began the same way. "You know I'm deeply committed to—shall I say—the evaluation of the Radford murder. So if you don't mind, just a question or two for completeness sake." It was an initial line of interrogation he'd often used on those he didn't strongly suspect of illegal activity.

Each man listened intently, Bateman once biting

his lower lip, Medicore probably faking a serious face in deference to a comrade in law enforcement.

Face-to-face with Bateman, he asked, “You ever have somebody come in here and act suspicious?”

“Over what?”

“Anything.”

The martial arts director looked confused. “I’ve got to know more than that, David. Over what?”

“Like too much criticism of Radford.”

“That was the norm, so I wouldn’t call it suspicious.”

“Sorry, Bruno. As you can see, I’m searching. Not exactly desperate, just searching.”

His interview of Captain Medicore was just as awkward.

“I’ve never interrogated someone like you before,” David said.

“What makes me so different?”

“You know: a police captain plus an old friend.”

“Now we’re friends.” Medicore winked playfully.

“We’ve always been friends.”

“You wouldn’t have known it during my first few months here.”

“But that’s when you showed up with …I’d say …a chip on your shoulder.”

“No way, David. I was just insecure—new on the job. Didn’t know what to expect. That sorta thing. But go ahead, like I was just an ordinary citizen. Ask me whatever you want.”

David had never heard him speak in those terms before and was most satisfied in hearing the captain's confiding remarks.

Ill at ease, David said, "Nah, that's enough about that, Nick."

Before leaving each man, the standard comments surfaced: "He was hated by most everyone," and "How did he ever become governor?"

David informed them that their responses were the norm among those he'd already talked to. Then he thanked them for their time, mentioned his was limited and, forgetting his ordinary half bow, excused himself.

Outside headquarters, he passed up his usual inspection of the flower garden, as he needed the time to drive to Greenwich for an interview with Jonathan Cartnagle, one of the top industrialists in the country. David had phoned him earlier about a possible interview, figuring Cartnagle's thinking might be shared by most of the highest income people in the state. Realistically, all of them couldn't be interviewed, and it was well known that this man was the wealthiest. It was also well known that he'd given large sums of money to Radford's campaign for governor.

David had also set up a conference with Radford's opponent in the previous year's election, Harold Bartow, a prominent Republican from nearby Stamford. David would drive there next.

The general upshot of the meeting with Cartnagle

was predictable but not its main disclosure. And Cartnagle was not reluctant to reveal it. That in exchange for over a million dollars contributed to the campaign, Radford, if elected, would appoint the industrialist's son Director of Economic Development. He had failed to do so.

When queried about limits to political campaign contributions, Cartnagle's reply was: "There are ways to get around it."

David was too tired to pursue the matter. He was just as tired when he arrived at Bartow's house. More of a large cottage than a house, it was situated on grounds with two secluded lakes, a walled kitchen garden and a vineyard.

Inside the front door, they skipped greeting formalities except for Bartow's opening lines: "I noticed through the window that you stopped to admire our flowers. Most people do. Anyway, welcome to our little 19th century abode. Come …sit."

"Thanks, Harold. I won't take up much of your time. First off, condolences over last year's outcome."

"Thank you. I'm glad it's over."

Of average size, he was younger than the usual gubernatorial candidate. And probably more handsome, with facial features and attire out of a fashion magazine for men.

They sat in a study with a rich but light-toned décor, its gray-blue cloth walls grabbing David's attention. As did an antique desk and, in a wall niche, shelves of bronze smoked glass that framed vignettes of objects––art, pottery, tortoise-shell, all arranged like small still-lifes.

"The color is seamless but the texture shifts," David said. "Very impressive."

"Emily and I think so. Sorry she's not here. Off shopping. But what's on your mind?"

"Well you must know by now that I've taken on the investigation of the governor's murder."

Bartow nodded but showed no change of expression.

"And I'm simply getting in touch with a sample of people connected to him in any way during the recent past."

"In my case, I would say 'disconnected'."

"In any event, what do you think about the case?"

Rather than providing a direct answer other than the ones David had been hearing all day, Bartow launched into a 15-minute diatribe about what he believed was wrong with the American-style political system.

He discussed his views on term limits, on campaign finance reform, on kickbacks, on voter fraud, and on what he termed "money power."

"Do you know," he said, "even foreign countries help U.S. candidates? But there's a better example of money power that involves a retirement community up near where you live—I think it's called Maple Village. It has four or five thousand residents housed in these gigantic condo blocks. All well-off people on beautifully manicured grounds. What does this oaf do? He pays for their grounds' maintenance for a whole year!"

"Really?"

"Yes, really." By now, Bartow was steaming. "So don't you think he eventually reminded all of them he was running for governor? That's a lot of votes."

After more critical comments, he repeated a former opinion that Radford had it coming, ending with, "I wish I'd had the chance to do it myself."

It was the first time David had heard such a wish.

On the drive home, he muttered "Spent and spend" more then once. It was another mantra that was among his long-held quirks—referring not to dollars but to fatigue and a desire to spend time with Kathy.

She met him at the door at 6:30. "I was worried about you," she said.

"Goddamn traffic on 84," he blurted and then cursed traffic lights, bad drivers and road repair crews.

"But why the worry?" he asked. "I've been home later than this."

"I don't know. Just a funny feeling."

Their hugs and kisses lasted longer than usual. In the vestibule and again in the kitchen.

"So how did the day go?" she asked.

There were glasses of wine already poured and waiting on a refrigerator shelf. She handed David the fuller one. He crooked his arm for her to take. She took it and led him into the living room where he tugged off his shoes, collapsed on his favorite Avalon chair and stretched out his legs onto a matching ottoman.

He began to speak slowly and as he sipped half the wine, then gulped down the rest, he sketched the day's activities with increasing speed, hardly looking at Kathy. When he reached the subject of the traffic jam on I 84, she said, "David! Listen. Slow down. You're trying to do too much in too short a time. No one gave you a deadline."

After dinner and two more wines, the phone rang and David answered it.

"Hello David?" It was a familiar voice edged with confidence.

"Yes. And if you're who I think you are, I can't believe it."

"This is Juan Carlos Saltanban."

"I was right! Saltanban!" David said, the effects of three wines teaming up. "But isn't it after midnight there in Gibraltar? You *are* there, aren't you?"

"Yes, I am. I am calling for two reasons. One, to apologize for hanging up on you today and two, to ask you a question."

Though still perturbed over what he considered a downright rude ending to their previous phone conversation, David calmly said, "I accept the apology and would be glad to answer your question, if I can."

"It is this: would you like to work for me?"

Chapter 10

An avalanche of sickening memories descended like a black cloud over David's head. Of Saltanban promises, Saltanban betrayals, Saltanban disappearances. They had all been colored over in the past dozen years, leaving an acceptable picture of change and rededication. The businessman's record had achieved that. But somehow, the idea of working for him under any circumstance was nauseating. However, Juan was waiting for an answer.

Finally David said, "Give me that again."

"Would you like to work for me?"

Somewhat recovered, David mustered up the courage to ask, "In what capacity would that be?" He tried hard to soften his breathing. And he couldn't help but think that this might be a ploy to distract him from the Radford Business.

"Here is what I have in mind," Juan said. "It is about Buenos Aires. I would like you to go there as an ambassador for my company or, better still, for me personally. It concerns what you told me earlier today: the call from that woman and what she said about the responsibilities of Nadim Maloof. I must say that she is mysterious—her name never came up in my conversations with the authorities who hired us to do the work there."

David pressed the phone closer to his ear.

"David, your title can be whatever you want it to be: ambassador, associate, colleague, whatever. In effect however, you would be doing what you have been trained to do and have such experience in: possible criminal investigation. You would be handsomely compensated. We can work that out if you give me reasonable assurance that you are interested in my proposal."

A few fleeting thoughts crossed David's mind: Joe Gomez who, when last heard from at Christmas time, was still the Deputy Chief of the Buenos Aires Metropolitan Police. He would be a good contact person. A phone call to him might suffice but it wouldn't come close to what would be gained by a direct visit to the city.

"Reasonable assurance of interest?" David chose the words carefully. "I can give that right now, Juan. But as for following through, I must give it some thought. You know, of course, that I'd have to put my analysis of the Radford case on hold here. I'm not sure that would sit well in many quarters, both here and throughout the country. I understand the murder and my investigation are making national news."

"Well, David, as long as you brought that murder up, there is reason to believe that the dagger used to kill your governor either came from Buenos Aires or was a facsimile of it."

"What's that? Say that again!"

"Whoever killed him must have somehow acquired the weapon from there. It may have been part of Eva Perón's artifacts, but believe me, I can't say anything further about it just yet because of Argentine security issues."

Again, David, shocked, thought of Joe Gomez. And Eva Perón's personal effects. "But I have no jurisdiction there," he said.

"That is not needed now. For what anyway?"

"For whatever I find."

"David, your role would not involve solving a murder there. It would be limited to what I have said: checking on that Cristina woman and Nadim's neglected responsibilities."

"You used the expression, 'criminal investigations' before."

"That is correct, but you can determine what Nadim had already done in terms of my company's obligations. And might I respectfully ask, are there not other crimes besides murder?" There was a slight pause before

Juan continued.

"Plus do not forget what I said before: while you are there, you would have the opportunity to check on the dagger used in your case in the U.S. How you handle it at your end is none of my business, but I would guess that if interested parties question why you are leaving the country in the middle of an investigation, you can say you have a lead on the weapon involved. I think that would justify your trip."

David had heard enough. Unexpected, but information worth exploring.

"Tell you what," he said. "let me think on it and I'll call you in the morning. Say about ten, our time."

"Got it. Is that not what you people say? I hope it will be good news for me. Now to bed. Goodbye, David."

"Wait! A fee? If I agree to go, forget a fee. You just take care of all expenses."

"No. That plus a token for your time."

David held that he was already receiving a fee for the overall Radford Business and whatever relevant evidence he might find would be covered by it. That rationalization notwithstanding, he said, "Only if you insist."

"Yes, I do. Expenses plus an extra ten thousand. If you find it necessary to stay longer than a day or two, I will increase it accordingly."

Kathy had been at his side during the entire conversation, her face reflecting shifting interpretations of how much she could hear. She could have picked up another phone but apparently feared a click might have given it away, plus David had never signaled her to do so.

He was quick to inform her of what had been said, almost word for word, he appearing gleeful, she on this side of doubtful.

But true doubt never materialized when she opined, "You've *got* to go, darling, much as I'd hate your being so far away. But the origin of the dagger is crucial."

"I agree. I'll first spread the word—among the people who count—that my leaving the country for a brief period is in the best interest of solving the case. But I won't mention where because this new approach would excite the media. They'd hound me and follow my every move. After that, I'll phone Joe Gomez about my coming down. I'll mention the Cristina call and the governor's being murdered with an unusual dagger. Then I'll look up Joe as soon as I get there. He'll be four-plus helpful. Make it five."

"Take Musco with you?" Kathy asked.

"I'd like to, but I'd better get Saltanban's okay first."

While Chief Gomez was fresh on his mind, David called him after all.

"Joe? Big surprise. It's David Brooks from the States."

"Wait a minute now. David Brooks in *person*?"

"Yes, it's me. How the hell have you been?"

"I have a stock answer for that, David, but first, how about you?"

"I'm okay, but what's your stock answer?"

"I'm absolutely fine for the condition I'm in." David made sure his laugh was sufficiently loud.

"Good. Listen, Joe, I'll be coming down there soon about some things I have to research. I'll look you up when I do. But in the meantime—and it's the reason I'm calling—what can you tell me about a certain Cristina De la Fuente, if anything? Do you know her?"

"Cristina? Oh yes, I know her. Everybody does around here. She's a troublemaker. Well known by us at headquarters because of all the complaints against her; none criminal, just being a nuisance. And a liar. All over the country I understand. Kind of a traveling bigmouth. And, David, are you ready for this?"

"Whatever."

"For a short time, she was married to the guy you mentioned in your last Christmas card."

"Who was that?"

"Nadim Maloof."

"Married?" David cried, uncrossing his leg and recoiling, all in the same motion. "I can't believe it! How long were they married?"

"Only two or three years. He probably couldn't stand her any longer and filed for the divorce."

"Does she work?"

"Yes, she does. Has for years. At the Roldan Auction House here in the city. Mainly fine arts and antiques. I couldn't swear to it but with her voice, she probably does some of the auctioneering herself."

"Hmm, very strange. Very, very strange. I'll explain when I get there."

Shortly before nine the next morning, a call came through from Cairo, Egypt. "*What is it with long distance calls?*" David wondered.

"Hello, David? This is Nadim Maloof. I'm in Cairo right now and I'm calling to ask a special favor of you. I can only imagine how full your schedule must be, but maybe you can squeeze something in, especially when you hear what it's about."

David said he'd be glad to hear what it was about but didn't know what was meant by "squeezing something in."

"It means flying here to Cairo because I'd like you to meet with two gentlemen—Japanese—who've already arrived to hear my special lecture the day after tomorrow. I'm really at my wit's end and I need someone like you to assess what they have to say and to determine if it's credible. You have the necessary experience and you're trustworthy and you're exactly what's—or should I say who's—required in a situation like the one I'm facing."

"Well thank you for the compliment, Nadim, but I'm preparing to fly to another country tomorrow." He didn't want to confuse the issue by identifying the other country. To say nothing about confirming the demands Cristina had spoken about.

If there's such a skill as interpreting silences, David had it. "I know you're disappointed," he said, "but making both trips would be one helluva squeeze."

"Unless you can delay the other trip. All you'd have to do here is converse with them. But maybe first attend my lecture, because I'll be covering some of what they mentioned to me. It couldn't be more serious if it's credible."

"And it can't be done by phone or email?"

"No, because you've told me yourself that body language is very important."

David felt stymied. He was curious but couldn't give an immediate answer. And his next question was the obvious one: "What will you be talking about?"

"Bio-engineering."

"Did they say it would be alright for me to be there?"

"Yes. I said you were a good friend of mine from the States and they approved of it. And when I said that would make it two against two, one of them said, 'That sounds like a battle. Which isn't what we seek. We seek a cooperative venture. A challenge to be sure, but at the same time, a mutually agreed-upon venture.' Something like that."

David was scrambling for a way out, filtering

various statements and questions through his mind. He made the mistake of verbalizing the wrong one: "You'd make the flight arrangements?"

"Yes, of course. You'll come then?" Nadim sounded as if he'd just made the winning score in a ballgame.

"I'd like to help out, believe me, Nadim. But let me get Kathy's opinion."

"It's vital you come, David. You see, and I hope this call isn't being monitored by anyone, my worry is in believing what they hinted at. Understand, it was only a hint. That in using legitimate bio-engineering techniques, the process could be altered in such a way that it becomes dangerous. They were more specific than that, but because this is a phone conversation, I can't elaborate just yet. But I got the feeling these two men want to consult with me on all of this in an ongoing way."

Nadim paused, then resumed: "Let's see, what else? I think you already know I've had an arm's length––and innocent—relationship with Japan's underworld, the Yakuza. But so do the two men and others they represent."

"Isn't this an affair for the police though?"

"If I go to them, I'm afraid I'd be killed. Remember: the Yakuza. Incidentally, I may be wrong, but the Yakuza and their counterparts across the globe—they don't bother with tapping into phones or things like that. They tap into each other—in person. A better way of saying it is that they spy in person, not electronically.

"No, not a police affair. It would take a person like you who might confer with the men after my talk and wander into the 'altering' subject. With your vast experience, you might be able to bring out what they're really thinking and detect whether it's serious or not. I guarantee you'd be properly paid for this and I don't believe it will take very long; maybe a couple of hours."

"Give me your number there and I'll call you right back."

Nadim gave the number, repeated it and said, "I'll be waiting, and I hope it's a go."

Luckily Kathy hadn't left for work yet and overheard David's last few sentences. "What was *that* all about," she asked.

When he paraphrased the conversation, her reaction was a brusque, "That's not exactly slowing down, my dear."

He countered with, "I'd like to help out, Kath. He sounded desperate and I really think the trip would be a quickie." Within an instant, he initiated a slow, steady stare, saying, "And speaking of quickies . . ."

"David, don't. I'm late as it is …and you know what I think about your quickies."

"No, tell me," he teased.

She didn't and, instead, they went ahead with it.

Afterward, David called Nadim back and agreed to cooperate as best he could. They settled on travel details and David learned the time and place of the lecture. He assured the professor he'd arrive on Monday morning.

Nadim indicated he'd arrange for a properly identified man to meet him at the airport and drive him to "the best hotel around." After David checked in, the same man would take him to Cairo University's Medical School, Kasr Alaini, or show him a few sights if they had time to spare.

David then waited until shortly before 10 a.m. and placed a call to Saltanban. Instead of giving an affirmative answer to the previous night's request, David said, "Is it okay with you if Musco Diller comes along?" It was a calculated opening. He definitely wanted Musco to accompany him and beginning that way would give the impression of its being a condition of his making the trip.

"Of course!" Juan said—a thunderous expression of thanks and approval rolled into one. "A nice man. I should have spent more time with him when you were both here."

"Then it's a deal. I'll need to spend at least the weekend here, contacting those needing contacting … you know, explaining my absence …and I'd be able to leave maybe Tuesday or Wednesday. Thursday at the latest." He didn't mention the Cairo visit.

During the all-night flight to Cairo International Airport, David spent most of the time trying to catch up on sleep. He'd never been to that Egyptian city before, so between naps he read an article in one of the magazines he found in the rear pocket of the seat in front of him:

> Cairo, the capital city of Egypt, has nearly 7,000,000 people, making it the most populated city in Africa. It lies in the Nile Valley at the southern lip of the Nile Delta. The Nile River divides into two channels just north of the city. Huge deserts lie east and west of the city. Some famous reminders of ancient Egypt, which include pyramids and the Great Sphinx, are located in Giza in the desert west of the city.
>
> Cairo is a mixture of the old and the new. The oldest and most historic sections are in the eastern part, the newer, more modern sections along the west bank of the Nile; on islands in the river; and on Garden City, a narrow strip along the east bank. Most government buildings, foreign embassies, museums, hotels and universities are on the islands or in the suburbs.
>
> A good many buildings in the modern sections were built in the 1900's in the style of present-day designs of America and Europe. These sections have many gardens, parks, public squares and wide

boulevards—all of which make these areas less crowded and more orderly than the older sections.

In sharp contrast, Cairo's older areas are famous for what's called their "old quarters"—areas of narrow, winding streets and buildings that are hundreds of years old. They're known for their more than 300 mosques (Islamic houses of worship). Minarets (tall, slender towers) are important features of the mosques. Islamic officials (called muezzins) announce prayer atop the minarets five times a day. At least one minaret can be seen from almost any place in the city's old section.

Cairo's museums house priceless treasures from many periods of history. The city's Egyptian Museum contains the mummy of Ramses II and the gold mask and other belongings of King Tutankhamen.

Many Europeans and some Jews live in Cairo, but their numbers have decreased greatly since the mid-1900's. At that time, the government took over most businesses and adopted policies that promoted the economic opportunities of

> Egyptian Muslims. These policies limited the opportunities of minority groups and foreigners.

David found the whole article informative, but an early sentence stuck in his mind: "Cairo is a mixture of the old and new." It reminded him of Nadim: the mixture of an academician and lately, a business entrepreneur.

The lecture was scheduled for 11 a.m., but though David had hoped to be early, his escort dropped him off in front of the medical school at 10:55.

After receiving directions from one of the white-coated medical students, David raced to the designated amphitheater and quietly entered via one of its uppermost doors. Before him was a "pit" not unlike many he himself had lectured in. Jam-packed, perhaps 400 individuals sat on the edge of their seats. He managed to find an empty one in the last row, near the aisle.

Shuffling some papers on the stage below, Nadim was perusing the audience, obviously looking for David. Spotting him, they smiled at one another and cast two-finger waves. Nadim looked impressively academic in a long white lab coat, all pockets stuffed with pens, pencils and, undoubtedly, lab reports. He was encircled by various audio-visual materials: flip charts, opaque and overhead projectors and the like.

He began the lecture by thanking administrative officials for inviting him and the audience for coming. Then he stressed that, for as long as he could remember, he preferred to make power-point presentations, with his words projected on a screen behind him. He reasoned that this made it easier for attendees to take notes—simultaneously "hearing and seeing" as he put it. At that point, a large screen rolled down at his back and overhead lights grew dim.

David didn't take notes but in the ensuing talk, he read more than he listened:

> Let us proceed. My official remarks will not take long but about 15 or 20 minutes after presenting them, I'll return here to take any questions you might have. Those few minutes will give us all a chance to freshen up, as they say.
>
> I'll begin by telling you what genetically modified foods are and then I want to discredit them. And you have heard, I am sure, about my recent interest in terrorism, especially bio-terrorism. I won't take up much of your time on it, but we'll end up with that.
>
> For some time now, genetic engineering has been making headlines in the field of nutrition and so-called food safety. It's the process of altering foods by removing a gene from one type of substance and inserting it into another type. Proponents of the process claim that

the result is greater quantities of a food product plus a fresher one. (For those of you not looking at me but at the screen, I'm snickering!)

I'll give you a simple example: genetically altering a tomato. Let's say it's too soft to begin with. It so happens that a naturally occurring enzyme, polygalacturonase—PG for short—makes tomatoes go soft. So through the genetic engineering process, the gene responsible for making PG is isolated and copied. It can then be ...quote ...reversed ... unquote, which serves to cancel its softening capability. This altered gene is next put into bacteria which are placed into a container with tomato leaf pieces. Little do the leaf pieces know that when the bacteria are absorbed, so is the new gene. The upshot of it all—if you'll forgive the pun—is that when the leaf pieces sprout, they're eventually transferred to soil. Then the seeds are collected from the sprouted plants and, voilà, the next generation will produce the altered tomatoes.

What about foods other than tomatoes? Well, I'll preface the answer by stating that genetically modified foods were first put on the market in the early 1990's. Yes, as early as that. Typically, these foods are transgenic plant products, such as soybean, canola, corn and cottonseed oil. Animal products have also been developed, although as of mid-2010, not one of them is currently on the market.

To give you an idea of what had been accomplished in this area, in 2006, a pig was controversially engineered to produce omega-3 fatty acids through the expression of a roundworm gene. Ugh! And researchers have also developed a genetically-modified breed of pigs that are able to absorb plant phosphorus more efficiently, and as a consequence the phosphorus content of their manure is reduced by as much as 60 percent. Ugh again!

And I haven't even touched upon changes in the smell of altered flowers. This is possible also.

But getting back to foods in general, critics have objected to modification on several grounds, including possible safety issues, ecological concerns and economic concerns raised by the fact that these substances are subject to intellectual property law.

I won't elaborate here, but I have problems with the whole approach and so does this country. In fact, importing or exporting any genetically modified foods is banned here. Implementing that in its entirety is a problem in itself, but that's another story involving politics, finance, ethical concerns, the size of our food supply and so on.

My own reservations concern food safety, transfer of food allergens, tampering with nature, domination of the world's food production by a handful of companies, and even the simple process of labeling: confounding the labeling of genetically modified crops with the non-modified.

So that's enough of that. I've presented it only because so many of you have written me about it.

Now how does any of this relate to bioterrorism? It doesn't specifically.

And why and how did a medical doctor become interested in the subject? During my earlier training in Japan, especially when I was on duty in a hospital there, I saw so many patients who had died or were near death as a result of

> some crazy people experimenting with biologicals that could do harm. I vowed that someday I would get involved—not in the way they did, but in opposition. I knew then and I know now that one person can't stop people like that. Some call them "terrorists". I call them "malcontents" because I believe a malcontent blossoms first and then he or she may evolve into a full-blown terrorist. Taken together, they form my current "interest model".

The screen rolled up, the lights brightened, and Nadim spent an additional 15 minutes on the value to society of scientific "interest models", citing the latest advances in stem-cell research, genome sequencing and cancer-gene testing.

He dismissed the gathering after reminding the students and others that he'd be returning to the stage within 20 minutes. He also asked that the two Japanese individuals who wanted his advice about a confidential topic meet with him in the room next door.

"No, not the one marked 'Restrooms'", he said. "On the other side."

The room on the other side was relatively barren and probably smaller than either of the restrooms. It contained a metal desk, a couple of floor lamps and six straight-backed chairs scattered about. Nadim was the first to arrive and he pulled four chairs together in a conversational square. Within minutes, David and the two Japanese men walked in and the usual formalities transpired.

Each Japanese man introduced the other: Jun Hirata and Shiro Mizuochi. Each spelled his last name. They looked like caricatures of Japanese guys out of old movies: eye slant, skin color, straight black hair, perpetual toothy grins. All but their size. These men were *big*—with big handshakes.

The crux of the meeting arrived when Mr. Hirata asked Nadim if he could offer advice regarding the modification of candy.

Nadim, in an apparent attempt at humor, responded by saying, "Are we bringing children into this?"

The two Japanese showed no emotion. After an extended silence, Mr. Mizuochi said, "No, the general public."

"But I don't understand," Nadim said. "Why candy?"

The two looked at one another before one answered, "To create something completely brand new. Never around before. Anywhere. A different flavor, a different taste, a different smell, even a different feel in the mouth." He inhaled dramatically and smacked his lips.

The other added, "Have you ever heard of such a thing before? I doubt it. Not with candy. Think about it.

We could corner the market."

More discussion followed, all centered on candy with an emphasis on changing what the world was used to. Before long, the two men were using the term "candy-engineering."

Throughout the meeting, David listened as intently as he had read the screen during Nadim's lecture. And he scrutinized each man's every movement, every gesture. As it turned out, he asked only one question during the entire session: "How many people do you represent or are you going this alone?"

The answer was unequivocal as one raised his voice to answer: "That is not important, sir. But to give you an answer, let's just say there are others."

His sidekick tipped his head to the side as an indication that they should leave. As they rose, he said, "We're really not in much hurry, gentlemen, but you'll get back to us?" He handed both Nadim and David a business card. "Maybe by mid-summer? We have important things to do in some other countries that will take some time."

"Yes," Nadim said. He inspected the card, front and back. "You'll definitely be hearing from me. Thanks for coming to my lecture."

"Not at all," Hirata said. "We enjoyed it. And nice to meet you, Dr. Brooks."

They left the room but David stayed behind.

"Well, my good friend, David," Nadim said. "What

do you think?"

"In a single sentence?"

"If that covers it."

"I'd call them thugs and they're up to no good."

"Smart thugs, though."

"We'll see."

"I was afraid of the 'no good' part," Nadim said, "but I wanted to hear it from someone else, especially you. Now what?"

David got right to the point as if he had scripted it ahead of time. Two points, actually.

"First off," he said, "They were quite clear about not being in a hurry so I'd wait awhile before contacting them. About what? That's the second point and I'm not putting you off, Nadim, but this whole scheme of theirs is potentially earth shattering—if they're to be believed. First candy. What next?

"What I'm leading up to is that I'll consult with that old colleague of mine, Paul D'Arneau. In my opinion. he's the world's leading expert in recovering lost or stolen treasures, but he also dealt with an emergency in Japan related to the sarin release in Tokyo in …I think it was 1995. In fact we worked together on it. Plus, I intended to call him anyway. About the dagger—a lost or stolen commodity, however you look at it."

"Well I'll be darned! There's that D'Arneau name again. When I brought up his name at the governor's wake last week, I never got into the history we shared.

But did I mention that he came to one of my lectures last year?"

"Yes, you did. And that he showed you photographs of me."

"Correct. At the time, he had a whole host of problems he wanted to discuss with me and we did that. I believe I was of some help to him."

Nadim appeared more tranquil than he had the whole morning.

"Isn't that ironic?" he said. "I'm asking for your help; your close friend once asked for mine; and now, he's going to help me."

"Hopefully the three of us can work this all out," David said, his fingers crossed.

In the school's cafeteria, Nadim indicated he would drive David back to the hotel after a lunch which he didn't enjoy, his concentration elsewhere.

Chapter 11

In a beachfront location at the edge of a secluded cove, the Ritz Carlton Sharm El Sheikh highlighted stunning pools and a large dose of glamour.

From the outside, it was shaped a bit like a wedding cake, its main building graduating upward in grand white swirls topped by a gold dome. Pure glitz. More so inside. The lobby set the tone with all its sparkling marble, opulent rugs and gold-topped pillars.

After showering David with thanks and appreciation, Nadim advised him to take an afternoon nap.

"I know all about your immunity to jet lag but you look tired. So do get some rest, have a nice meal—one's been paid for in the central restaurant—and in the morning, that same man will be here at six for your plane ride home."

David agreed to all of it, returned the thanks and pointed to a side lounge.

"That cherry-wood bar," he commented. "I've got to say it wouldn't look out of place in a gentlemen's club. Think I'll precede the dinner with a wine or two right in there."

"I'd suggest going in after dinner. At seven, a musical quartet starts playing and they're absolutely terrific."

"Another good idea. And, Nadim, let's keep the lines of communication open. Regarding our Japanese friends, call me whenever, and I'll do the same from my end."

David did take a nap. He couldn't recall the last time he'd done so. And if it were meant to energize, it was a dismal failure, for even repeated cold water splashings to his face failed to erase a lagging stupor. He didn't know if the cause was hunger, the complicated investigation, or what he had once coined as "PNS"—Post Nap Syndrome. It was why he normally only slept evenings.

He elected to tackle hunger while trying to rid his mind of multiple investigative details, although he was more inclined to visit the lounge and have a wine or two. But he remembered what Nadim had said about an excellent quartet arriving at seven—it was now six—and decided to have dinner after all. It turned out to be an unexciting meal and he wondered if not having a wine yet had anything to do with it.

Promptly at seven, he drifted into the lounge just as the quartet started playing. He thought the music was too loud and the room too crowded but, believing he'd get accustomed to it, found an empty stool at mid-bar. He sat, but before having a chance to order his drink, he stiffened at what felt like the muzzle of a gun pressed against his back.

"Yes, it's a pistol," a man whispered in his ear, "but don't look around to find out."

David remained still, save for a brief dip forward when the pistol dug in deeper. He wondered if this were some sort of trick or the real McCoy. Either way, he was in no mood for it and was tempted to retaliate. But he wasn't sure how.

"Now get up real slow," the man said. "I'm putting the pistol in my pocket until we get to our car. You follow along with us, see. Stay real close and don't make a scene or you're a dead man."

David complied as two other men materialized at his side. Neither appeared to be carrying guns. He noticed that all three were Japanese but shorter than the ones he'd met at the university.

"A day of thugs?" David murmured, most of which was drowned out by the music.

"What's that?" the armed assailant asked.

"Nothing."

Outside, they walked as a unit. David glanced

back and saw the man directly behind him withdraw a pistol from his pocket and hold it secretly under his open jacket.

"It's six or seven cars up ahead," he said. "Just keep walking …nice and easy."

On the way, David recalled what he was once taught: that if he were accosted by an armed man and ordered to travel elsewhere with him, he should definitely resist. For the chance of survival is higher by fighting him off on the spot than by being driven to another location.

Three men but only one is armed.

They were halfway there. In less than an instant, his past training in karate and bujutsu at Bruno's Studio flashed through his mind. He had toughened his hands by pounding padded boards; progressed through back stance, cat stance and forward stance; mastered the front kick, hook kick, roundhouse kick and side kick; learned the two-finger and knife-hand punches; become an expert in proper blocking, striking and falling. He had well earned his black belt.

Pick the right moment.

At a dark car with dark windows, the armed man opened a back door and said, "Get in."

Now!

David took a small step to the rear, rammed his elbow into the man's abdomen, twisted around while falling to the sidewalk, and in *tomoenage* or circle throw, swung the man over the top of him. The pistol tumbled off to the side.

By the time the man was helped up by the other two and the pistol was recovered, David was off and running. He ducked into the nearest alleyway and headed toward the riverfront. Turning, he saw the men in quick pursuit, though nearly a block away. Occasionally, David ran in zigzag fashion in case a shot were fired.

His senses on the qui vive, he didn't fail to notice heavy storm clouds overhead and a pale moon.

But he suddenly lost sight of his pursuers and the discovery struck him with a terror that had gradually been building from the start. He could feel the perspiration crawling across his stomach.

Several minutes later he reached the river's edge. A sign with an arrow pointing left that read, "Back to the Lovely Ritz Carlton" could be made out on a stanchion. Its light cut through wisps of vapor usually seen at daybreak. The sound of a nearby foghorn startled him and he ran faster. He had expected a fishy smell but chalked up its absence to his breathlessness. And then the rains came, heavy and steady, soaking the earth, producing deep, swift currents on the cement walkway and macadam road.

David hoped the thugs had given up the chase because of it. At least for the moment. Were they waiting to pounce on him from any of the many doorways he was passing? He paused ever so briefly before approaching each one, at the ready for more karate moves.

He had seen several individuals on the way down but practically none as he plodded on through the driving rain.

It was the same for cars—from several to almost none. However, he kept a sharp eye out for anything moving that was dark, either people or cars.

He moved quickly along after pulling up his wet collar and the lower part of his trousers, looking around in every direction, but so far, no one was in sight. He slowed down as the raindrops began to feel good on his sweaty face and hands.

Finally at the hotel, he walked cautiously through a side entrance and up to the front desk.

"Do you have a security guard on call?" he asked the clerk.

"Yes, we have two. Is there something wrong?"

David, uncomfortably wet, restrained a smile and related what had taken place over the last half hour, leaving nothing out.

Currently without the aid of his Beretta Cougar .45 and Seecamp .32, both disallowed aboard airplanes, he felt deeply at risk and asked if a guard could accompany him to his room. One was summoned and escorted him there.

David had an urge to contact Nadim but with five mysterious Japanese in the picture, decided not to. Instead, he double-locked his door, dried off and slept fitfully for most of the night.

He spent an otherwise boring flight back to the U.S. filling a new notepad with what had occurred during the encounter with Nadim and particularly, Mr. Hirata and Mr. Mizuochi. It was all for use in his explanation to Kathy plus as a reminder of events that had been added to those already clogging his brain.

He wrote: "If I had only known what would develop in just ten day's time, I wouldn't now be flying back from Cairo and then almost immediately leaving for Buenos Aires." He even included a watered-down version of the chase.

David arrived home in Connecticut, late morning, U.S. time, and though feeling sluggish, went directly to Kathy's office at police headquarters. They embraced for what seemed like an eternity. Then he withdrew the notepad and read what he had written word for word. She listened attentively.

When he had finished, he said, "So that's over. Now I'm off to Argentina in the morning. I just can't believe I'm doing this."

"What?"

"Country-hopping."

"You asked for it."

David regarded her sternly. "Not really," he said. "I hadn't bargained for *this* kind of travel."

"Well, darling, I have news for you."

"Now what?"

"Thatcher Drinkwell called. Wants to hear from you

as soon as possible."

"The guy from St. Helena? The one Paul D'Arneau raves about?"

"That's the one. From what he said, you may have to go there."

"There? St. Helena? No way."

David stroked his head at the temples for a full ten seconds.

"Okay," he said, "what's the reason?"

"I didn't understand half of it, but he said something about Japan and the sarin attack back in the nineties. And then he went on and on about his bad experiences in discussing sensitive subjects over the phone. Like being bugged. Or resorting to shortwave radio where signals are bounced off the ionosphere—I think he called it. He said if that were the case, the whole world could listen in."

"I know I'm repeating myself, but I can't believe this is happening. You mean to tell me that he wants me *there*?"

"That's my understanding. You'd better call him, but call Paul to begin with."

David was the first to admit that he was always confused over time zones, especially when great distances were involved.

"You know," he said, "I think you're right. And I don't give a damn what time it is in St. Helena or Argentina. Or in Timbuktu for that matter. I'm calling now. Well, not exactly now because I need freshening up. So I'll make both calls from home."

"Better check with Paul first, David." She served up the advice like a warning.

David knew that Paul still lived in New Haven and could just as easily have driven there as made a phone call. But time was at a premium: there was still contact to be made with Thatcher Drinkwell in St. Helena, and then the long-delayed trip to Buenos Aires beginning in the morning.

David hadn't spoken to Paul since Radford's murder, neither one having called the other. But that's the way it always was. They had an unwritten agreement that one wouldn't bother the other unless advice was sought. Advice that was always sincere and well thought out.

Years ago, it hadn't taken more than a couple of drinks at a bar midway between Hollings and New Haven for them to iron out the pros and cons of confiding in each other over current and upcoming cases. Good-naturedly, they often argued over whose plate was fuller–—a criminal investigator's or a treasure hunter's. But one thing had always been clear: either one could contact the other at any time, day or night.

They'd also agreed to dispense with the usual preliminaries during calls—covering health, family, the weather and the like.

"David, old buddy," Paul said, "Good luck on the

challenge you've taken on."

"You want it, Paul?"

"No way. Seriously, are you making progress?"

"Slow but sure. Lots of travel involved. In fact, I'm leaving for Buenos Aires in the morning." David tried hard but couldn't suppress a yawn.

"Reason I called though: I just got back from Cairo where a couple of men brought up a subject you're more familiar with than I am. Your old perfume case and the Tokyo sarin attacks?" David, not thinking clearly but undisturbed because it was Paul at the other end, had put it in the form of a question but wasn't sure why.

"I remember it all clearly, David. How can I help?"

"Cairo Chemical. Wasn't that somehow involved?"

"Yes, it was. Listen, I'm at my desk right now. Give me a minute to get to one of my file cabinets and I'll bring back the folder on all this stuff. I can read you what I summarized at the time."

That was another thing they frequently jostled about: which one kept the more complete notes.

Paul returned within the minute.

"I found it," he said. "You want me to read the whole thing or just the essentials?"

"What's essential to you may not be to me and vice-versa. And what's essential to me may not be to you and vice-versa. So better read the whole thing."

"Ha-ha, very funny. Know what?"

"What?"

"You'd better catch up on some sleep."

There was a protracted silence before Paul finally broke it. "Okay, here it is, word for word":

Subjects Brought Up at Cairo Chemical with Tarek Ronque

—Said they have 2 divisions in their complex: 2 chemical plants and a training unit.

—Said most employees are chemical analysts and the facilities are aimed toward improving chemical products rather than creating new ones.

—His main function is to implement an Egyptian Non-Lethal Weapons Directive (NLWD). They instruct students in an advanced chemical, biological, radiological and explosives training program. Teach them on-site and in the field.

—He listed titles of some of their courses, but stressed two: "Vehicle Borne Improvised Dissemination Device Prevention" and "Improvised Dispersal Device Construction and Disassembly." Emphasized the words "Dissemination" and "Dispersal."

—Used the sarin nerve gas incidents in Tokyo subways as example of long-range delivery devices being converted for short-range purposes.

—In connection with NLWD, he said that “non-lethal” could be used as a cover.

—Said chief reason why he asked us there was to talk about a man who called with unusual request. Man said he was “worldwide perfumer”. Wouldn’t give name. Referred to CR-23, Aut-45 & ERE-12. Tarek explained they are 3 chemicals that can make other chemicals disperse better. But not suitable for perfumes. The 3 are manufactured only at Cairo Chemical. Tarek emphasized it is very expensive to do so.

—Man wanted to buy the formulas for them. Would use them as additives to his company’s perfume lines so their perfumes would disperse better then competitors’.

—-Tarek refused, saying the 3 chemical additives are too powerful for perfume dispersal. Key point of whole subject matter.

—When asked why Cairo Chemical manufactures the 3 in the first place, Tarek said it was commissioned to do so by Egyptian government.

—Tarek also said Thatcher Drinkwell wants us to visit him on St. Helena. Still vague over phone but did say concerns Hiroshi Inoue who consulted him about a certain poison substance.

—Thatcher insists we go. What a trip! But will go. Sooner or later.

––Tarek knew all about stolen perfume packet.

—I brought up our plans to visit Egyptian temples. Talked us out of it.

"So there you have it, David. Are you still awake?"

"I guess so, but I'll be in better shape to digest it tomorrow or the next day."

"Come on! You'll probably forget most of it by then. Tell you what. You go ahead with your Argentina plans and I'll put this in the mail pronto. That way you'll have it when you get back."

"You're a peach, Paul."

"I keep telling you that."

"But don't call me one," David said. "Somebody's liable to hear you and it's not a very good moniker for a criminal investigator."

"It's a deal."

"So you went to St. Helena. That I know. Should I go?"

Paul wasted no time in answering. "By all means. You'll love Jamestown. That's the capital and it's a village like no other. But more importantly, Thatcher Drinkwell will be invaluable. He's the constable there. A treasure-trove of information and . . ."

"Leave it to you to express it that way," David interrupted.

"Meaning?"

"'Treasure-trove'. It's probably in every treasure hunter's vocabulary."

"Why not? You guys say things like 'That's criminal' when you're referring to things as innocent as a grocer throwing out one-day-old peaches."

"There you go with 'peaches' again. But we're getting off the subject. You think it's worthwhile to make the trip, then?"

"No question about it. It's a long way, but you're used to distant travel. As I said, the guy knows his stuff. And he knows just about every histarian there is. He's one, himself."

"Histarian? You mean historian?"

"No, histarian. It's a long story that would take me all day to finish. I'll leave it up to him to explain it better."

"I see. And you think Drinkwell would help me with what I'm facing?"

"Yes, and in all its ramifications. I'm sure there are plenty."

"Please don't get me started on that. It's another thing that would take all day."

David suspected Paul had more to say about St. Helena's constable.

"If and when you go," Paul said, "you'll soon find out why they call him the 'Component Constable'."

"And why do they?"

"Because he explains everything in components."

"Who's 'they'?"

"Anyone who consults with him. And he doesn't shy away from the designation. He should have been a scientist, not a law enforcement official—so precise, so organized—almost rigid in his thinking. Won't take you long to discover it for yourself. Take his notes, for example. The ones about his components. They'll drive you crazy. He must spend hours putting them together."

"Now I can't wait."

"So you're going?"

"With your enthusiasm about it, how can I resist?"

"Great. You won't be sorry. Let me know how you make out."

"Of course."

"And while on people you might want to visit, there's another one I saw and was glad I did. He's a prior in southeastern France—name's Frère Dominic . He's getting on in years but, like the constable, he's an histarian and knows what he's talking about. He's an expert on Napoleon who, as you know, may have died from arsenic poisoning. He'll bring up the subject and give his views on how it—and other chemicals for that matter— how they can be slowly released into the atmosphere and kill by inhalation. Definite insights.

"But I should warn you. Don't be shocked if you find the prior very long-winded. His favorite topic is wars. He can list the important ones from memory and can spiel them out almost in chronological order. He thinks even the old wars are related to every aspect of current life in one way or another."

Paul presumably took time to size up David's possible reaction before saying, "You'll go there, too?"

"I'd better. And, you know, just like the constable should have been a scientist, you should have been a travel agent."

David eased the phone away for a moment as it was hurting his ear. Returning it, he said, "An observation of mine, Paul. I noticed you stressed the word 'vague' in reading off your notes."

"You picked that up, didn't you? Well, the point is that he *has* to be in his position as constable. What with all the electronic equipment at his disposal, apparently everyone and his brother can tap into his conversations. So nothing's a secret on the island—at least nothing involving him. But no one listens in to nobodies like us."

"I hope it stays that way, and I don't like *that* moniker either."

David knew the conversation had gone on too long but decided to introduce the subjects of Saltanban,

Cristina and even the dagger. He only scratched the surface in each instance but believed there might come a time when he would seek advice about them from an outside source. And who better than Paul?

David believed the call was one of the most productive he'd ever made. He was particularly anxious to hear more about so-called histarians from Drinkwell and was surprised to hear him say that Nadim was one of them. Since Paul had indicated that many work anonymously—David took that to mean "undercover"—he wasn't sure if he'd ever broach the subject with him.

Early in the phone call to St. Helena, Thatcher Drinkwell said, "We've never met, David, but I've heard all about you and I'm impressed."

"Thanks, and consider the compliment returned."

"Paul D'Arneau told me you do the work of two or three men, but I decided to call because the information I intercepted the other day sounded like it needed attention by someone like you. Or like Paul.

"But you've had more experience in dealing with out-and-out criminals. And those sending the messages sound like criminals to me. Actually, I feel so strongly about this that I'd come there to talk about it, but I'm the constable of the entire island and have no replacement. No one here is qualified."

Drinkwell held back a moment as if he were weighing his next thought. "Want a job?" he said.

"Right about now, I'm tempted to say yes."

The constable's laugh induced a coughing spell. Finally he managed: "I'm sure. Anyway," he continued, "I'll explain. And it's in the form you'll need to translate because I'm always being spied on electronically—phone, shortwave, you name it."

"Let's give it a go."

"You know, I really like your responses. Short and sweet, just like Paul's. You're like two peas in a pod."

"Not again! First a peach, then a nobody, now two peas in a pod."

"What's that?"

"Oh nothing. You were about to say …"

"Let's see: how to go about this. What we'll cover if and when you get here—and I pray it's 'when'—has to do with certain items you and Paul know about from before. The real expensive ones? Plus the thing you're looking into at your end …ah …the extent to which these items come into play and your recently begun …uh … search? Well, they may be related."

David didn't know if the references included the Cairo Chemicals dispersals, the dagger, the Radford murder itself, or all three. But since he felt his primary obligation rested with the murder case and there was a good chance that was what Drinkwell was alluding to, he immediately said: "Constable, hold on. I don't want this fouled up. I'll be there."

"Super! That's a relief. Since you're not here now,

may I have your drink when I toast the decision later?"

"Yes, by all means. Make it drinks if you want. However, I must explain. I leave for Buenos Aires in the morning so I'll be tied up a bit. And the man who works with me half the time will be there, too. Name's Musco Diller. May he continue on with me?"

"I have a suggestion," Thatcher said. "Why don't the two of you come here directly from Buenos Aires? First going home and then flying here is almost twice the distance. Or looking at it another way: coming directly here from Argentina is a little more than half the distance. I can arrange the flight through the R.A.F. I've used them many times before."

"Good point. I'll give it some thought." David had responded as if consideration of flying logistics didn't deserve priority status at the present moment. But he didn't dismiss it; he would simply file it away for now, check with Kathy later, and come to a decision later in the day. He so informed Thatcher.

"I understand. But just so you know, David: the R.A.F. chaps and I are very, very close. Sometimes they accommodate me with very little advanced notice."

"Who pays for it?"

"No one really. It's a question of favors for each other. They fly for me in effect; and I advise them on the latest advances in telecommunications."

"Some kinda deal," David said.

"It is, and both sides benefit. Now, about our present

situation, their pilots fly quite often out of London's Brize Norton airbase to the Falkland Islands, sometimes swinging by Ascension Island and landing there. It's about 700 miles north of us. They could do the same thing coming from Buenos Aires. Then you'd board the Royal Mail ship, *St. Helena,* for a day-and-a-half sail to here. I'm thinking that would give you a wonderful break—a good time to rest up."

David thanked him, said he would phone later, then immediately recollected what the two Japanese men had said: that there was no hurry in getting back to them because they'd be busy until the summer. And David didn't want to bring up such a time element.

"May I switch the subject a little to see if you're ready for a question, constable?" he asked.

"Yes, of course."

"Who would win a medal for losing the race, a turtle or a hare?"

"Turtle."

"Correct. I was made aware of that recently and was told 'Besides, the hare had other things to do'."

Before they exchanged best wishes, David expressed another disguised thought. The real meaning was, "It's like we're in a contest. Who's the more indirect?"

He was confident that Drinkwell's experience rendered the translation an elementary one.

Chapter 12

Once in Buenos Aires, David lost the headache he'd had most of the way down. It was intermittent but pounding, lessened only by his trying to force attention away from the murder case he'd been commissioned to investigate. A case that featured many typical forensic circumstances but also the stabbing of an atypical man with an atypical weapon.

On the way down, it had dawned on him that, although Kathy was in favor of a later trip to St. Helena, he'd forgotten to mention Drinkwell's suggestion about flying directly from Argentina, bypassing a return flight home.

But essentially this was a goose chase to determine the weapon's origin, among other things. He hoped it wouldn't be too wild a chase. It was primarily the weapon, an elaborately constructed dagger, that had convinced him to make the trip in the first place. For Saltanban's statement that it may have originated in Buenos Aires had to be looked into. And if that were true, why had it later turned up 5,000 miles away? Or was Japan the point of origin?

At the airport, he stopped to read a small wooden-framed plaque about the city, remembering the one just outside the Gibraltar tunnel, but with less lingering anxiety over what he had endured—although in some ways, he felt just as much frustration. Who ordered the captivity? What's with those Japanese thugs? What's in store in this Argentine city, often called "The Paris of South America?"

Musco read along with him:

> Buenos Aires is the capital and largest city of Argentina and the second largest metropolitan area in South America, after Sao Paulo. It is located on the western shore of the Rio de la Plata, on the southeastern coast of the South American continent. That is where you are now.
>
> Greater Buenos Aires conurbation, which includes several province districts, constitutes the third largest conurbation in Latin America, with a population of

> around 13 million. The city is the one most visited in South America. Its inhabitants are referred to as *porteños* (people of the port). It is known for its European style architecture and rich cultural life, and has the highest concentration of theatres in the world. Do visit one or two. You will not be disappointed.

Musco asked, "What's a conurbation"?

David shrugged, "I guess it means a collection of something."

Musco thought a minute, then said, "So we're hunting for a . . ." He looked at the plaque again, " …for a conurbation."

David chuckled for the first time that day, then became straight-faced.

"Let me apologize right up front, Musc," he said. "This is a beautiful city, frankly one of the most beautiful I've ever visited. But we're on a mission or two, not a sightseeing tour. So you wouldn't think I'd be shortchanging you if we just tend to business, would you?"

"Fine. I'm okay with that."

Wasting no time, they hailed a taxi and headed straight for the headquarters of the Argentine Federal Police. It turned out to be an eclectic structure with influences from Baroque architecture, according to the taxi driver who had never stopped giving the history of every building they passed.

David hoped his friend, Joe Gomez, wasn't out on assignment.

Inside, David identified himself as an American counterpart to Deputy Chief Gomez. He had stretched a point slightly. Even more so when he designated Musco as his lieutenant.

The receptionist indicated the Chief was in his office, and led them up a winding staircase to a wide office door before ushering them in.

David and Joe tried to muffle shrieking that they hadn't seen each other in years and then shook hands as if in a battle of strength. Joe repeated the process with Musco.

Gomez, in full uniform that included several gold and silver badges marking years of service, looked more North American than South American: tall, straight-backed, fading blond hair, bright green eyes. Almost clean shaven, he had a row of punctate scars across his jaw.

David waved a finger in their direction. "From a fight with thugs?" he asked. The word was still fresh in his mind.

"What? Oh, those. No, nothing that exciting. From a fight with skin cancer. Basal cell. Not the type that spreads anywhere."

They sat comfortably, Gomez behind a maple desk

that appeared too small for his expansive though cluttered office; David and Musco on deeply cushioned chairs not often seen in police surroundings.

"You know," Gomez said, "sometimes coincidences are hard to figure out. I was going to phone you later today after we finished some investigating. A man showed up yesterday at about five. Japanese fellow. Said he was here on your behalf—he gave your name—and asked if *all* of Eva Perón's personal belongings were on display or were there more kept somewhere else? Said he'd already explored everything in view at Museo Evita. He stressed he came here all the way from Cairo, where he was visiting. Like he was looking for sympathy."

A muscle along David's jaw tightened. The trip was already paying dividends.

"Did he give his name?" he asked.

"Yes, I have it right here."

The Chief flipped open a file folder he'd taken from a shelf behind him.

"Let's see. He goes by the name of Shiro. That's his first name. Refused to give his last, as I remember. I also asked him to spell the name he gave me. That's when I got a little ticked."

"How come?"

"He said, 'Just like it sounds, sir. S-h-i-r-o'. Kinda sarcastic-like. Imagine! Guy marches in here, asks a bunch of questions, won't give his last name. And acts like that?"

David shook his head before mentioning, without going into detail, that he had met a man with that first name in Cairo. But he never gave the man permission to be his representative.

"I coulda socked him," the Chief said angrily. "Anyway, he repeated he was here on your behalf, but he was really employed by someone in Tokyo. Wouldn't say who or what about that either."

Gomez closed the folder and flung it back on the shelf. "You, by any chance, know of this guy?" he asked.

David replied, "No, I don't," even though he wondered if the man in question could have been one of the two men he'd met after Nadim's lecture. "What did he look like?"

"Japanese. Only big. *Very* big."

"And did he say where he was staying?"

Gomez reached for the folder again. "Yes, it's all down here. But before I forget, when I told him I wasn't sure about other belongings, he suddenly got polite and asked if I could ask around and said he could be reached at the …let's see . . .the InterContinental Nordelta Tigre. If you're not familiar with it, David, it's one of the finest hotels we have—the only one that can be reached by land or river."

"For rapid getaways," David joked. "Only kidding, Joe."

"No, that was good. And you're still fast."

"I don't know about that. By the way, is there more to Evita's collection?"

"Yes, I know that for sure, but I didn't want to commit to the guy before I researched him some."

"Did you?"

"Not really, but I've thought about lots more questions to ask him before going to that trouble."

David thought this presented the perfect opportunity to meet up with possibly the same man he had met just days before.

"Maybe we could call on him in his hotel room," he said. "I say 'we' if you wouldn't mind if we tagged along."

"On the contrary. We could do it right now. And I think it's best to show up without calling ahead."

"Let's go," David said with an imploring half-smile.

All the while, Musco had been taking notes, inconspicuously as usual.

The Chief drove a blue patrol car up to a gated community in the Nordelta district, waving to every police officer they passed, David nervous in the passenger seat. He was itching to see if this Shiro was the one he'd met. He and Gomez nicknamed him "Shiro of Cairo."

Musco sat in back, straining to observe swimming pools, soccer and tennis fields, medical buildings, churches, schools, playgrounds, saunas, a telecommunications center and the Tigre Museum.

Foregoing the parking garage and pulling up in front, Gomez made only one comment before they entered the hotel: "I'm not sure what it really means, but they say this place is a balance between modern style and nature."

David was impressed with what he interpreted as poetic.

The Chief saluted the concierge and various uniformed employees before striding to the main desk, a wall's length of Argentine paintings plastered on its front surface.

"Ah, it's you, Flavio," Gomez said to the lead clerk who hailed him as "Mister Chief" while interrupting the registration of a guest and his family.

"How you doin' and how's the family?" Gomez asked.

Flavio fashioned his thumb and forefinger into a circle.

"Very good. Listen, we're on official business. Can you see if there's a Shiro somebody registered here?"

The clerk checked a nearby computer and said, "Yes, he's registered in Room 206. And I remember waiting on him myself. Real big but it was the smile. He never stopped smiling."

"Did he give a last name?"

"Not really. When I asked for it he said to put down 'Shiro Shiro." Paid cash up front, so I did just that."

Now David would have bet his life that the man was

the "Shiro of Cairo."

Gomez continued with his questions. "Have you seen him today?"

"No, not today. Or yesterday, which is the day he arrived here."

The Chief's puzzled expression mirrored David's.

"As I said before, Flavio: official business. I can now label it police business. Can you or one of your assistants take us to his room without calling ahead?"

"Absolutely. For you, Mister Chief, absolutely. I'll have to get back here fast because we're shorthanded today, but I'll take you there myself. There won't be any trouble, will there?"

"I hope not," Gomez said.

At the door to Room 206, he whispered to the clerk, "You knock; we'll stay behind you. When he comes to the door, just say he has some visitors and we'll take it from there."

When there was no response to repeated knocking, the Chief said without explanation. "You must have master keys on you. Please unlock the door." He lifted the covering of his side holster.

The clerk promptly unlocked the door and scampered off.

Inside, a large-framed male body was crumpled on the floor against an easy chair. David swallowed hard, realizing there was no mistaking it as the body of Shiro Mizuochi and that he was dead. A small spatter of blood was clotted on the carpeting between the body and chair.

The three exchanged dark looks. Gomez then spoke with authority:

"I'll have to report this immediately of course, and the crime scene unit will arrive here soon, but David, this is the stuff of your career, so go ahead, do your own checking first." He said it as if he knew nothing would be disturbed from a forensics standpoint.

"Thanks, Joe," David said simply. He walked over to the body and, with one finger, felt for a carotid pulse, and found none. He noted that the lower part of the head was purplish while the upper was waxy pale.

"Any chance you have any surgical gloves with you?" he asked the Chief.

"No, not on me, but there are some in the kit we store in the patrol car. I'll be right back."

In the meantime, David continued his inspection, "old hat" to him, keeping his hands in his pockets. He knew the Argentine team would be taking smears for fingerprint, DNA and other analyses. He also knew what to look for.

A slender ribbon of dried blood was caked across the right shoulder and at the back of the twisted head was a small round bullet wound with blackened, seared margins: an entry wound. There was no larger, irregular exit wound.

He looked around the single, rather bare room but

found no gun or spent shells.

Sniffing audibly, he thought he detected an unusual odor but couldn't place it. A woman's perfume?

Musco examined counter surfaces, chairs and cabinet tops, his hands clasped behind him.

The Chief returned and handed David the gloves. "That was fast," he said and thanked him.

David snapped them on and carefully lifted Shiro's head. It was cool to touch. There was stiffness in the muscles of the neck and jaw but none in the muscles below. He pressed his fingers on the purplish-colored aspect of the head and there was no blanching.

What David had done thus far was second nature to him: a preliminary crime scene reconstruction. All that was left was also second nature. He asked for the chief's patience before leaning against a sidewall and, while staring at the body, tossed around some mental sequences. He gesticulated now and then with the fingers of both hands.

Musco sat motionless. He had witnessed the practice before and didn't say a word.

Off in a corner, Gomez was busy making the phone call to headquarters.

David formulated the following:

Body cool to touch. About 10 degrees temperature lost.
Early rigor mortis in small muscles of

neck and jaw.
Early fixed lividity with no blanching.
Therefore, dead 4 to 6 hours.

High-velocity impact spatter on hand.
Therefore, hand in close proximity to
head when shot.
Protection?

Edges of entrance wound black &
seared.
No tattooing or soot smudge.
Therefore, hard contact by gun muzzle
against skull.

Round rather than stellate entrance
wound.
No exit wound. Bullet still within skull.
Therefore, probably .22 caliber handgun
used.

All this took less than five minutes.

"You want to stay while the unit's here?" the Chief asked David.

"No, I've seen what I have to see. Clear-cut murder. I think he lifted a hand at the last minute. Reflex to protect himself. And why a .22, I'm not sure. Probably an amateur, not a hired gun."

"But what leads you to believe it was a .22?"

"Because if the bullet lacked the velocity to penetrate bone a second time—I mean from within, at the other side of the skull—instead ricocheting around within the skull cavity, then a .22 is a good bet."

The Chief, visibly impressed, said, "I see. Makes sense."

"An X-ray would verify it, but I'm reasonably sure the autopsy will show the bullet lodged somewhere inside."

"I'm sure," Gomez said. "I'd better notify the people downstairs."

He went to the phone and cradling it at his neck, described what they had found while, at the same time, scribbling in his notepad.

A six-member team of police officers and lab personnel arrived a short time later. The Chief briefed the lead officer as best he could, introduced David and Musco, then preceded them down two flights of stairs and out to the patrol car.

This murder of a mysterious Japanese "thug" as he still considered him, dead or alive, did little to change David's hankering to view more of Evita's other private belongings, if there were any. And he was well aware the Chief was in the best position to help out.

In the parking lot at the rear of police headquarters, he invited David and Musco up to his office but David declined, crossing his legs and getting comfortable.

"Talking here in the car will do, Joe. Unless you have things to tend to up there."

"Yes, plenty, but this is important."

All three took out notepads simultaneously. Upon noticing it, each laughed quietly.

"Maybe when all is said and done, we can combine our notes and write a book," David said.

"We can call it, *Deadly Politics*," Gomez said.

"Or *Deadly Business*," Musco chimed in.

David felt obligated to render an opinion and said, "Or *Deadly Political Business*."

It was an interlude that broke a stark silence during their drive from the murder scene.

"Now," David said, "in my phone call to you, I mentioned a conversation with a Cristina what's-her-name. Since then, I've learned all about her. A fraud, really."

"That's about it."

"Well no doubt you'd have trouble dealing with her, but could you set up a meeting between the two of us while I'm here?"

"No problem. I have to talk to her anyway because she's first on my list as Shiro's killer."

"You think so? Right now I'm open-minded." To those asking, it was a common declaration early on in many of his murder cases.

"But did you notice what could be a perfume smell in the room?" David didn't wait for an answer. "Also, a woman's more likely than a heavyweight to use a .22."

"Perfume? Yes, I thought so, too. But maybe Shiro was …ah …entertaining other ladies in his room, not necessarily his killer."

"Maybe." David folded his hands before his lower face as if in prayer. "This is getting more interesting by the minute." He let his hands drop to his lap.

"Let's get to Evita's belongings now. I forget where I heard it but I understand they couldn't fit all of them in the Museo Evita. And Shiro wanted to see any leftovers. You know where they might be?"

"Yes. They're locked up in a basement room at the Casa Rosado—the Pink House. It's our executive mansion and I can get a master key right there. That's where people think Eva Perón gave a passionate balcony speech before thousands of cheering fans who packed the Plaza de Mayo. But it really never happened except in the Madonna movie. You know, when she sings, 'Don't cry for me, Argentina'."

"I remember the movie," Musco said. "Saw it three times. She should have won the Academy Award but she didn't because she's Madonna."

"Can we go there now?" David asked.

"Certainly."

They sped off to the back of the Pink House. Gomez parked the car in a space marked "Privado."

At the end of a canopied and flower-lined walkway, they entered a huge round room with a cement floor and cracking walls. It was enveloped by a series of closed doors. Except for one.

There, in an open doorway, an older woman sat reading a newspaper. She looked up and said, “It’s you, Chief. May I help?”

“I hope so, Rosa. And how have you been?”

“Why complain?”

Several more questions and answers ensued which David had difficulty hearing. Finally the woman produced a large chain of keys. She plucked one off with ease and pointed it at the nearest door.

The three men smiled their thanks, Gomez unlocked the door and they walked in. Several lights automatically flashed on.

Piled before them in about 20 tabled cartons were articles of all sorts: clothing, jewelry, cosmetics, silverware, books, photographs, candles.

A single table was prominently labeled in Spanish. David cocked a questioning head toward it.

“It says, ‘Not to be displayed’,” Gomez said.

“Okay if I look through it?”

“Go right ahead. I’m curious myself.”

David dug in and soon remarked, “Everything in here is in pairs.”

“Yes. They must be the things Evita’s two bodyguards donated to the Peróns. They were with her constantly—the same two while she was in power. Personally, I’ve never looked through the box.”

As the chief peered over his shoulder, David

extracted a pair of silver badges in a small container; two similar belts tied together; and various medals, epaulets and insignias. Next was a pair of pistols and their scabbards. They were wrapped in pink twine.

And below them was a single strand of twine.

"No dagger!" David exclaimed. He had a haunted look. "Where can it be then?"

"I have no idea," the Chief said. Then his eyes circled slowly in their sockets.

"But wait," he said with increasing excitement. "I remember hearing that one of her soldier guards may still be alive and living in the city. A Fernando Morales."

"Really?"

"Hmm, let's do some figuring," Gomez said. "I do know Evita died in 1952—in other words, 60 years ago. She was First Lady for six years before that. If Morales started as one of her guards in his early 20's, that would make him about 85 or 86 now."

"Worth calling him?"

"Let's give it a try."

They returned to Rosa and asked if she had a phone book and if they might use the telephone on her desk.

"Yes and yes," she replied.

The Chief found a number for a Fernando Morales, dialed it and held the phone inches away from his ear so that David could listen in.

A strong voice answered.

"Fernando?" Gomez asked.

"Yes?"

"This is Chief Gomez from police headquarters."

"I didn't do it," Fernando said.

"No, no, nothing like that."

Gomez then explained what they were trying to find and were having no luck.

The former guard said, "I can help, chief. At least I think so. For some reason—I'll never know why—the Peróns didn't want the daggers kept with her things. The guns, yes. But the daggers, no. So they gave them back to me—a pair of them."

"You have them then?" Gomez corrected himself: "I mean one of them."

"I had the pair for awhile but then Cristina De la Fuente …you must know her; everybody does . . ."

"Including me."

"Well, she came to me and asked for them. I gave them to her …should have asked for something in return, but when she told me what she needed them for, I decided to give them to her for free."

"When was that?"

"Recently. Maybe a month ago?"

"And what did she need them for?"

"You know that she's a big shot at Roldan's. Said she wanted to offer them up for auction with some other famous things. That the bidding would go on and on and whatever money was taken in would be donated back to the Museo Evita. Anyway that's what she told me, and that's what I did."

On their way back to the car, hardly a word was said, as if all three knew what their next move should be.

Adjusting his seat belt, David said, "That makes our interview with the ever-popular Cristina that much more important."

The Chief obtained her telephone number by contacting headquarters. He phoned her and she agreed to meet them there in half an hour.

The three men arrived first and when Cristina walked into the Chief's office, David's immediate impression was that she didn't totally deserve the reputation that followed her around.

She was a striking woman of about 50 with a figure of one about thirty. Tall and statuesque with seldom blinking blue eyes, her hair was swept back in a classic chignon. Its color featured an edgy rainbow of expresso, gold and auburn.

David stared at her face but even more so at what she was wearing: a short raspberry silk waistcoat embellished with gold, over a pale lace sheath embroidered with hundreds of tiny flowers made of pastel sequins.

She seemed bent on mischief as she introduced herself to each man individually, dwelling the longest on David.

"Good to put the face with the voice," she said. During that time, he detected no perfume fragrance. No rings. Little to no makeup. And no jewelry except for ruby earrings.

“Thank you for coming with so little notice,” Gomez began. “And I’m sure you’re as busy as we are, Cristina, so let’s right to the point. We understand you have in your possession one of the daggers that once belonged to an Evita bodyguard and . . .”

“That’s crazy!” she snapped.

Gomez continued as if he’d heard no reaction. “ … and that you may be offering it up for auction.”

“Crazy; just plain crazy.”

David made a permissive gesture toward the chief who nodded his approval. “Do you know a Fernando Morales?” David asked.

“No.”

“Well he’s the guard who told us.”

“Pure garbage,” she responded. “Garbage! Anyway, why would I do such a thing if I had it?”

“He said you’d donate the money received back to the Museo Evita.”

“Well, that’s a nice thought but that man misled you.”

“Switching then,” David said. “What you said before while we were shaking hands …indicates you remember your call to me?”

“Of course I do. I made it, didn’t I?” She had become a different person in a matter of minutes.

“About Nadim Maloof, right?” David inquired, after a brief hesitation.

"Right. I said he wanted money from this country plus some of Evita's artifacts. Period."

"That sums it up," David said, not eager to reveal the denials of both Nadim and Saltanban.

"Do you own a .22?" he continued.

"What's that?"

"It's a gun."

"I don't own *any* guns, sir."

Cristina was making no effort to hide her agitation.

"Well," she said, taking over, "for your information, I've since heard that good old Nadim would be willing to give up his demand for the money in exchange for definitely getting the artifacts. And if that's all you have to talk about in dragging me down here, gentlemen, I have better things to do, so good day."

She bolted from the room.

They stared at one another in disbelief.

"Phew," David said. "what a woman! Kinda off her rocker, I'd say."

"See?" Gomez said.

Musco hadn't bothered taking notes. Instead he observed the rapid interplay with full attention.

"Well that's that," David said.

"We didn't learn very much," the Chief added.

"Yes and no," David said but didn't verbally elaborate. As was so often the case in other interviews, he thought that once Cristina's body language came into play, it spoke volumes.

He informed Gomez that he had two phone calls to make and would have to leave.

"Make them from here. You could use the phone in the next room."

"But they're both over a great distance. I can reimburse you for them. One's to St. Helena where I'm headed straight from here."

"Don't be silly about reimbursement. Go and make the calls. And you're traveling way out there?"

"Afraid so and, you know, I'm tired of thanking all the time, but I'll take you up on my not paying for the calls."

"Consider the thanks made and take your time."

In the call to Kathy, relief could be heard in her voice: "I was so worried."

"Why the worry? I said I'd call."

"But I didn't even know if you arrived there safely. You *are* in Buenos Aires, aren't you?"

"I think I am."

"Think?"

"There's so much going on that …oh, you know what I mean. And you're okay?"

"Okay, but busy."

David then spoke about the people and things he'd come across in a relatively short time: Chief Gomez; the Shiro of Cairo murder (David could tell Kathy was shuddering); the absence of a dagger at the Pink House; Evita's bodyguard, Fernando Morales; the strange meeting with Cristina De la Fuente.

He saved Drinkwell's suggestion for last, stating he hadn't heard the suggestion on this trip but had neglected to inform her of it while still in the States.

"So it would be a direct flight from here to St. Helena with the R.A.F. Maybe I could spend a day relaxing here before leaving. Like on a guided tour of the city; maybe take in an opera; who knows?

"Then, I'd have at least a day on a mail ship from an island north of St. Helena—it's the island where the R.A.F. lands. That would give me even more relaxation time. And incidentally, it wouldn't cost a cent. They have a longstanding agreement which I'll explain when I get home."

David was dragging out the details, fearful of receiving a negative response, but he was thoroughly surprised at what she said.

"That would be *wonderful.* Good thinking on his part. And you know, darling, I have a suggestion of my own."

"Which is?"

"Why not ask him if you can fly with the R.A.F. wherever you go from now on?"

Chapter 13

David phoned Thatcher Drinkwell and first straightened out all the particulars involving the Royal Air Force's assistance. They both agreed that, taking the landing at Ascension Island and the Royal Mail ship's voyage into account, he would arrive in Jamestown in two days, give or take half a day.

Musco was delighted that he would be going too, and not returning to Connecticut on his own.

An R.A.F. plane would pick them up at Ezeiza (EZE), Buenos Aires' International Airport, and fly them to Wideawake Airfield on Ascension Island in less than three hours. It happens to be a joint facility of the United States Air Force, the Royal Air Force and the BBC World Service Atlantic Relay Station.

While writing this all down, David remembered reading that the airfield was used extensively by the British military during the Falklands War. It also brought to mind his once working on a criminal case involving both air forces.

Then after an estimated two-hour wait, they would set sail on *St. Helena,* the mail ship, and arrive in Jamestown, 700 miles and 36 hours away.

David considered the mail ship junket a reprieve from the rigors of over-thinking, over-remembering and over-doing. He mustered all his will to relax for over a day, and it worked.

There were about 40 other passengers they mingled with and, when not sleeping, exchanged stories with. Musco talked about books on municipal traveling and David on flowers, never on crime.

Well into the trip, David picked up a flyer from a table near the ship's galley. It was titled *St. Helena and Napoleon.* He was about to put it back down because he was as tired of reading flyers, abstracts and plaques as he was with handling phone calls. But, as always, he couldn't resist:

> St. Helena, a British Island in the south Atlantic, is situated 1,200 miles off the coast of Africa and 700 miles southeast of Ascension Island. The Portuguese discovered St. Helena in 1502 but it

became part of Great Britain in 1673.

The island is approximately ten by seven miles, about half the size of Napoleon's former home-in-exile, Elba. Rough and mountainous, it is composed mainly of volcanic wasteland. The highest peaks—Diana's Peak and Mount Actaeon––rise more than 1,000 feet above sea level. An area of past volcanic activity is Sandy Bay which contains fertile soil, ideal for the island's fruit and vegetable production. Three columns of Basalt in this area are called Lot, Lot's Wife and Asses Ear.

The island's only port and village is Jamestown, the capital. Its population is about 5,600, principally Europeans, Africans and East Indians. Its main bay is called James Bay.

The chief crops are flax and potatoes. For a century or more, the flax was used to make mailbags for British Post Offices, but this process has declined because of the availability of cheaper synthetic materials. Other industries there include fish curing and the manufacture of lace and fiber mats.

For many years, it was an important port of call for Portuguese sailors to replenish their supplies and to receive medical attention.

At one time, both the British and the Dutch claimed the island as their own as they visited it on their voyages to India. In 1659, the East India Company colonized the island. Fourteen years later, the Dutch attacked and took it over, but the British retook it within six months.

Napoleon Bonaparte of course was its most famous resident. After his defeat at Waterloo, he signed a second abdication at the Elysée Palace. Three weeks later, he surrendered himself to the captain of *H.M.S. Bellerophon* which took him to Plymouth. From there, he embarked on the *H.M.S. Northumberland* bound for St. Helena, arriving October 15, 1815. He was allowed a retinue of 30 people. Napoleon stayed at a small house, the Briars, while his eventual home, Longwood House was being readied. Shortly thereafter, he moved into Longwood and lived there until his death.

Three frigates and eight other vessels continually patrolled James Bay or were kept on standby. Gun emplacements and guard posts were established throughout

> the island.
>
> A year later, Sir Hudson Lowe was appointed governor of St. Helena and it quickly became apparent that he and Napoleon had little respect for one another.
>
> Napoleon died there on May 5, 1821. The cause and manner of death remain in dispute. Some claim he was poisoned by arsenic, either intentionally or by accident. Some even believe he inhaled the chemical from the coloring of his bedroom's wallpaper, having slept in the room for nearly six years. Others state he died of stomach cancer as did his father.
>
> He was buried in the island's Sane Valley where his body remained until 1840. It was then transported to Paris and currently lies in the Hotel des Invalides.

Approaching the island on a Monday morning, David was taken by the shape of it. From a distance, it looked like an enormous black iceberg with an irregular upper border and a thin valley down its middle.

They disembarked on—appropriately—Napoleon Street, the only street in town. With whitish buildings on either side and brightly colored cars moving slowly in each direction, the contrast was striking. The sidewalks were as crowded as the street, its residents immune to their presence.

They walked a short distance to the center of town, and registered at the Consolate Hotel. It was an 18th century building with wrought-iron balconies filled with pots of yellow and pink flowers, a quiet bar, and even a computer off its lobby. Drinkwell had reserved a single room for them with twin beds.

After rolling their own luggage to a room on the first floor—it was only a two story structure—they took turns freshening up and unpacking part of their belongings. They changed into similar clothes: printed short-sleeved shirts, light khaki pants.

"I'll take the bed closest to the door," Musco said, "just in case."

"Just in case what? Who knows we're here?"

"No. Just in case we have to escape fast," Musco said with a straight face.

David threw a pillow at him.

As it turned out, they flipped a coin, David won, and he selected the bed away from the door anyway.

The room was small but airy, with windows lining the back wall. Musco made sure they were all locked.

"You're still worried, aren't you?" David asked.

"I'm always worried if we're on ground level."

Back at the front desk, David referred to a card he'd taken from his pocket and asked the receptionist if he could arrange for a taxi to take them to the Police

Service Building.

"Ahh… where Thatcher Drinkwell practically lives," the receptionist said.

"From what I hear, I'm not surprised."

"And he's always busy."

It was about 10 o'clock when they entered the building, a single vehicle parked out front. Old and dust-laden, it was similar to the station wagons once popular in the U.S. The building itself resembled a rural post office more than a police station.

The weather had turned hot and humid with a temperature of about 80. They both put on sunglasses.

There were two rooms inside. An outer one contained little more than a desk, three chairs and a filing cabinet, all metal. Jetting out from one side was a holding cell, its bars uneven and scruffy. One bar was missing. But despite the room and its appearance of wear and tear, it smelled antiseptic.

David heard intermittent clicking coming from the back room, the kind he associated with the electronic equipment of command posts in police departments.

A man of average height and weight sat at the desk, scribbling something on a lined piece of paper. Maybe age sixty or so, he had closely cropped brown hair, brown eyes and a sun-baked complexion. A pistol could be seen strapped within a leather holster attached to the right side of his belt. He wore blue jeans, and his short-sleeved shirt was as brown as his hair and resembled those worn by the military, minus any epaulets. But he did wear a shiny badge.

A nameplate on the desk read: “Thatcher Drinkwell, Constable.”

“Constable?” David said.

The man looked up, hunched his shoulders and smiled easily.

“Well, I’ll be,” he said, a touch of doubt in his voice and manner. “You got here earlier than I thought. David and Musco, right? Even with those sunglasses.”

They removed them.

“Right,” David said.

Drinkwell rose, weaved around his desk and shook Musco’s hand.

Then he shifted to David saying, “Here’s what Paul and I did when he first arrived.”

Before he had a chance to do anything, David said, “I know. He told me.”

They wrapped their arms around one another, squeezing hard.

“And did he tell you what I said to him?”

“Yes, he did.”

“Give up?” Drinkwell said.

“Not a chance,” David replied.

“There, it’s now somehow official.”

David didn’t quite understand but offered, “Looked like an initiation rite to me.”

“Good way to put it,” the constable said. “Do sit.”

David dragged two chairs closer to the desk while Musco took out his notepad.

"You don't mind if I take a note or two, do you, constable?"

"No, not at all."

"Good," Musco said. "Some people think it's like eavesdropping so I always ask ahead of time …unless I forget."

"So did you get to relax any on the ship?"

"Just what the doctor ordered," David said.

"And the plane ride was okay?"

"Better than that. Which reminds me. Before we get to why we're here, I'll get something else out of the way. This is courtesy of Kathy, my fiancée."

"And that is?"

"Well, let's see how to phrase this. For the remainder of my current case, which seems to be taking me all over the globe, would it be an imposition to ask if we can fly with the R.A.F. whenever possible?"

Drinkwell didn't give it much thought. "Absolutely. And forget the 'whenever possible'. They have teams I can count on, so all it would take is a call from me."

"Excellent! She'll …we'll …be happy about that. I've got to tell you, Thatcher, those pilots …they're fast, they're on time, they're not nosey, and they're fun to talk with."

"Amen."

Already, David was impressed with the constable's

even disposition, all business but pleasant.

Each man then leaned forward almost imperceptibly.

"Alright," Drinkwell said. "The reasons I've asked you here?"

"Do some of them involve candy, by any chance?"

"Yes, candy. How did you know?"

David went into detail about his conference with the two Japanese men in Cairo, and also included his finding one of them murdered in Buenos Aires.

"Murdered? See, serious stuff."

But the constable, in effect, sloughed it off. "Anyway," he stated, "I'm guilty of doing what I complain about all the time: listening in on short wave conversations. In this instance, it was Tokyo conversations. They apparently don't disguise as well as we do. They were talking all day about the need to modify candy, of all things, but I'll get to that later."

Drinkwell then took out a batch of papers from a bottom drawer and spread them across his desk.

"Much of what I'm about to say is material I already shared with Paul when he was here. Did he tell you?"

"I'm not sure what you're referring to, constable."

"Oh, of course not, but it's all down here. I've added more and changed them around since then. God help us if the people I talk about ever get hold of these notes, especially my Components. And speaking of Paul, he filled me in on much of what you're going through right now."

He rearranged the papers to his liking and said, "That's what I call them, men: my 'Components'. So, let's begin."

He moved the top paper closer to the center of the desk and half from reading it, half from memory, said: "Component number one: the histarians."

"I hate to interrupt again, sir, but do you mean historians?"

"No, histarians. They're individuals located in practically every region of the civilized world and can provide information that can't be gotten any other way. Very few know of their existence and they give out facts only to other histarians or to those who come highly recommended. Very often they provide insights that are contrary to what history has recorded so they're appropriately named. Not contrarians, but histarians. I'm proud to say I'm one of them."

Musco began writing faster, licking his pencil point more often.

David remained silent for a moment, having heard Paul refer to them briefly during their recent phone conversation. But finally he did say, "You forgot to add that some of them like to remain anonymous."

"Yes, like the person I'm sure is our mutual friend, Nadim Maloof. We've never met, but since we're both histarians, we've spoken by phone."

David feigned surprise. "Nadim is one? Well, I'll be

damned! I must say, I'm both impressed and encouraged to hear about that."

"Impressed, I understand. But why encouraged?"

"Because my knowing about it makes me feel more positive about what he says."

"More trusting?"

"Yeah, that's a better word."

"Trusting about …about what?"

"Oh, about things I never heard of."

"And people?"

"And people."

The constable registered a look of uneasy puzzlement.

"And you're no doubt wondering," he said, "if Nadim is an histarian, why did he need you to evaluate those two Japanese gentlemen and to see if their scheme was credible? In other words, why was it necessary for you to go to Cairo?"

"Correct."

"Because that scheme was considered pure conjecture and therefore the opinion of other histarians wouldn't apply. He knew that, so he probably never called any."

"So if I read you right, you …they …never offer a definitive opinion without first checking with others of your kind?"

"Hmm, that 'of your kind' makes us sound like related weirdos. But I get what you mean, and the answer is yes. The histarians are constantly checking with one other in addition to delving into things with their own critical eye.

"Some claim we have mystical powers. We don't have anything of the sort. We simply do exhaustive research. 'Private collections from private collectors', we call it. And our sources are never revealed, but our conclusions always turn out to be right. Totally right and totally accurate.

"We have sort of a code we live by—'canon' might be a better word—'Never give out any information unless you'd die over its accuracy.' As applied to the case of Nadim which I just cited, we rely on solid factual information, not on opinion—although sometimes we'll express an opinion supported by the same opinion of other histarians, usually more than three or four. Four is the general rule.

"Who are the ones who've followed your travails––to more of an extent than you might realize? Well, there's Nadim. And yours truly. And some you've never met, but they know you very well. As an aside, I wish Paul D'Arneau would join us, but he's too busy with his worldwide travels. He is, however, very cooperative and reliable. I say it this way: he responds but doesn't initiate.

"Now, as for seasoned histarians, Frère Dominic at the Cistercian Abbey Notre-Dame-de-Senanque is someone you must see."

"Yeah, Paul mentioned him."

"He's up in southeastern France—Gordes. I can easily arrange for a flight to Avignon, 20 miles away. He's probably our top histarian, and our oldest. This may be the last year in his position there. Sort of long-winded but very keen. That reminds me, we all swore we'd never give out much by phone, only in person. I guess I hold the record for giving out the least over the airways. Paranoid I suppose, but that's me." He looked unapologetic.

David had heard about that too.

"Before we leave the subject of seeing Frère Dominic—Paul also speaks highly of him—would you characterize our seeing him as imperative or simply because we could get there easily from here?"

"Imperative," Drinkwell said firmly. "And the reason is that it has to do with arsenic. Arsenic and Napoleon. And that will be my next Component."

At the mention of arsenic, David came to an immediate conclusion. "So we'll go then," he said. "Like always, you can make the arrangements?"

"I'd be happy to, and I'm happy you didn't waffle over the decision."

The constable shifted the paper to the side and replaced it with another.

"So Component number two: arsenic and Napoleon. A while ago, a man by the name of Inoue called me, asking for information about Napoleon's dying from arsenic poisoning. He wouldn't divulge why he wanted to hear about it from me. Incidentally, I should say that I later checked with one of our Japanese histarians who told me his full name is Hiroshi Inoue and that he fancies himself as another Shoko Asaharam, the Islamic extremist and founder of the Arm Shivrikyo cult.

"Next, I'm going right to Component number three and you'll see why it ties in with number two. I happen to know you're familiar with the chemicals CR-23, AUT-45 and ERE-12. For purposes of our discussion, CR-23 is the more important. And it is *extremely* expensive. You'll see later why this is also important when I tie it all together."

Drinkwell stopped to read them several lines from his notes:

> In a sense, it acts like arsenic. If it's added to a nerve gas—sarin, for example—it can disperse the gas better. But, more than that, a person who inhales CR-23 must have more of it just to live. Like arsenic! Just like, possibly, in the case of Napoleon who it's said, inhaled arsenic from his bedroom wallpaper all the while he lived at Longwood, on this very island. Not too far from here in fact. Six years. So imagine if the two are inhaled. You have twice the danger and they both have to be inhaled in increasing amounts. Bottom line? Double the chance of death!

"Here's a better section," the constable said. "Well, maybe not better, but another way of putting it:"

> In Europe, arsenic was once used by some as a mind-altering drug. In small doses, whether ingested or inhaled, it produced a feeling of well-being and strength. When a person has once begun to indulge in it, he must continue to indulge ...or the last dose kills him. Indeed, the arsenic user must not only continue his indulgence, he must also increase the quantity of the drug, so it is extraordinarily difficult to stop the habit; for as the sudden sensation causes death, the gradual cessation produces a terrible realization that the user must continue to take arsenic until he or she dies.

By then, David and Musco were almost unnerved, as was Drinkwell. But he went right on.

"And here's the last about this before I get to Component four where I tie it all together. Then number five will deal with my recommendations."

> If the intake of arsenic involves only one episode—again whether by ingestion

> or inhalation—the effects indicated above can in many cases be duplicated if CR-23 has been added to it.

Musco stopped taking notes and peeked in David's direction.

During the clatter of the commander's paper shuffling, David whispered in Musco's ear: "I bet you're wondering what in hell all this has to do with the Radford Business."

Musco whispered back: "You read my mind."

"You'll see. Before long, what we're doing … as complicated as it may seem …traveling all over the place, and so on …it'll all make sense. I hope."

"Ready for Component four?" Drinkwell asked.

They both nodded.

"The way I tie it all together has some merit, I believe. Certain Japanese are up to no good. No doubt some of this evil group …let's call them that…are the same ones who were involved with sarin nerve gas 17 years ago. They don't want to resort to that kind of gas again because the authorities would be ready for it. In what way, I'm not sure. In fact, this time around, the evil group is trying to conceal the whole thing by turning to foodstuffs in general. And a further camouflage on top of that: candy. They're trying to generate a cover for arsenic!"

The constable had spoken rapidly and appeared not only deeply concerned, but winded.

"That's how I see it," he said. "As a doctor, you do know the symptoms of arsenic poisoning, don't you, David?" Ostensibly, he so inquired in order to create time to catch his breath.

And it worked, for the question brought David back to the days when he'd taught a forensics class that dealt with homicides by acute poisoning. It also allowed him temporary refuge from the commander's frightening scenario. He slowly pieced together an appropriate answer.

"I'm afraid I do," he replied. "Acute arsenic toxicity is due to its effect on many cell enzymes which affect metabolism and DNA repair. Symptoms usually start within 30 minutes and there's a characteristic sequence of multi-organ failure: neurological, cardiac, respiratory, renal, liver.

"Even if someone survives the initial sequence, bone marrow suppression develops after a few days or weeks. Not a pretty outcome. And for this to be deliberately foisted on a large segment of the population is hard for me to imagine."

"Me too," Drinkwell said. "But to finish up on this Component, gentlemen, Paul told me you know that Cairo Chemical was the only company that made that very expensive chemical CR-23. But about ten years ago, a Tokyo firm began making it, too—just as expensive. Maybe more so in this day and age. Cairo's still at it though. The Tokyo firm helped your governor's political campaign with cold, hard cash in exchange for his directing funding for the chemical from other U.S. sources. Then he called a halt to all such activity everywhere, as you know. Well, this arsenic idea is their way of retribution."

David had already assumed much of this, but not all. His reaction was worded as another assumption: "Paul's been helpful in giving you some background, I take it, Thatcher?"

"Very. He really should become an histarian."

"I agree."

"You should, too."

"Me? No way. No disrespect, but my plate is overflowing as it is."

"Maybe someday?" Drinkwell asked as if he were pleading.

"Maybe someday."

Once again, Musco's body language was easy for David to interpret. He promptly returned to the issue at hand.

"So who do you think the Japanese group wants to target?" he asked. "The U.S.? Egypt?"

"I think it's both, especially your Connecticut area."

"But Radford's dead now."

"Not his deeds as they look at it. And not his advisors. I don't really know. That's where Frère Dominic may come in. I only know the plan sounds real."

David began rubbing his decision scar.

"And one other thing in this fourth Component of mine. I almost forgot. The Japanese Yakuza may be called upon to help."

"The underworld?"

"Yes, the Japanese version of your Mafia."

Hearing that was almost like a last straw. "Christ, as if we don't already have enough," David whined.

"You know, Thatcher, this all started out as—I wouldn't call it routine—but as a single murder. You've no doubt heard from Paul and others that I hesitated to take it on. But I did. Then, day-by-day, it's escalated to where it is now: a devilish, all-encompassing challenge. Do this; do that; remember this; remember that. And, truthfully, I wonder if I'm still up to it."

"You're up to it," the constable assured him. "I'd swear to it. I feel I've known you for years. People have told me about you. Whether you realize it or not, you've been thoroughly probed. The histarians, remember? What you call a challenge, they call a cause célèbre. One to be taken up by you, and to be resolved by you. It's as if you've been ordained to be in the position you find yourself. So hang in there. Do I dare say please?"

It was the first time David had felt so overwhelmed by the escalating negatives of the case and his own discouragement. But also by the intensity of someone's confidence in him.

He reached over and shook Drinkwell's hand.

"Thanks, Thatcher. I needed that."

"Now then," the constable said, "my last Component—number five: my recommendations. I'm not even touching the Argentine element, even though I've been brought up to date on it. But I'll leave *that* up to you."

The recommendations had been written on a 4 x 6 card which he withdrew from his shirt pocket.

"It's more or less an outline, an obvious one at this point. Nothing complicated. You can add the nitty-gritty when you get around to it. But, in general, I've indicated what needs to be done."

He handed David the card written in ink:

1. Frère Dominic. Must see him.
2. Harry Shapiro of *The New York Times*. Must see him. Very bright and current. You and Paul are familiar with him. Better in person than on the phone.
3. In the end, pure and simple: the right people must be alerted and the evil group must be brought to justice, even if nothing has occurred yet. The main instigators must be named.
4. The scheme must somehow be brought out into the open. Let others do it. Maybe Shapiro can write another article in *The Times*.
5. The dagger issue.

After David had read it over, Drinkwell said: "That last item, the dagger? I'd say, forget about it. Who cares? Let it go. If it turns up, fine. If not, so what? That's my feeling anyway. Of course I'm referring to completeness. If there's something about the dagger that's crucial, then go for it. Otherwise, don't waste your time.

"You know as well as I do that often in law enforcement circles, they speak of relevant completeness and irrelevant completeness. Based on what I know, this is irrelevant completeness."

David put the card into his own pocket, saying, "Much appreciate it."

Before commenting any further, he thought that it was one thing to hear anyone's recommendations but quite another to follow through with them. The constable's, however, jibed with what David had put together in his own mind but hadn't begun to implement yet because they were incomplete. For the Hartford murder and the Argentine issue had to be brought into the picture. They had to be part of the overall implementation.

And finally, he thought that anything involving life and limb—in this case, an arsenic attack—had to be double-checked. Even triple-checked if possible. Frère Dominic, Harry Shapiro and another conference with Paul D'Arneau loomed large in this regard.

With double and triple still on his mind, David got up and said, "I give you double and triple thanks,

Thatcher. You've been extremely helpful."

Musco voiced the same opinion after also rising.

"It's been my pleasure and my duty, gentlemen," Drinkwell said.

They again shook hands. In a display of Musco-style humor, he also shook David's hand, and was the only one who smiled over it.

The constable resumed the conversation. "I figured you'd want to leave tonight, so I went ahead and booked you on the Argos. I don't know why but it's much faster than the mail ship you came here on. It's a small Greek freighter that hauls roll-on/roll-off vehicles, packaged lumber and containers. It's got cabin space for 12 passengers. It's comfortable and well furnished and sets sail for Ascension Island at 9 p.m. You'll be the only passengers on it."

"Good," David said. "And the R.A.F.?"

"There'll be a plane waiting on the island to fly you to Avignon, France. Then all that's left is the 20-mile drive to the monastery for your visit with the prior. He'll be expecting you. I assume you won't be with him for more than an hour?"

"That sounds about right."

"So I'll have the pilot wait for you at the airport. Maybe have another breakfast."

No sooner had David and Musco boarded the Argos at 8:45 than they noticed they were probably not the only passengers. Seated at the wheel of one of the hauled vehicles was a man with distinctive Japanese features. He was completely motionless, save for his eyes, checking most of David's whereabouts.

An hour into the journey, David approached Jake, the lead crew member, and said, "That man in the car over there. He's not part of the crew, is he?"

"No. Where'd he come from anyway?" The crewman looked puzzled. "I'll go find out from him."

David watched as Jake and the man spoke to one another for a full five minutes.

Jake returned and, shaking his head as if confused, said, "He maintains he got permission to sail with us from the embassy in Tokyo. I questioned him on it and, out of nowhere, he produces the same kind of document you gave us on boarding. Said he forgot to hand his over to us."

"It's none of my business," David retorted, "but wouldn't a stranger have been noticed by somebody from your crew team?"

"Not necessarily. We were told by Constable Drinkwell that you and your friend would be the only passengers. You arrived early so no one was paying attention to anyone else boarding after you. I guess it was our error but we did get the necessary document after all, thanks to you. Late, but here it is, with a Japanese insignia across the top."

For the remainder of the sailing, the man never left

the vehicle and never took his eyes off David.

Dockside on Ascension Island, he and Musco tended to their luggage, then looked around for the stranger. He had vanished.

Chapter 14

During the flight from the island to Avignon, David tried to nap, but was regularly awakened by feelings of both concern and anger. Concern over another example of his being monitored, and anger that it was happening in the first place. He tried to put the feelings aside, not only because he needed the rest, but also because he wanted to be fresh during the upcoming meeting with Frère Dominic.

They rented a car and with David at the wheel, began the 20-mile drive to Gordes, a medieval village that David knew had served the Resistance well during World War II. Three summers before, on a beach at Cape Cod, he had twice read a most interesting chapter in a book titled, *War and Beauty*. The setting was this very region and, as a flower aficionado, he marveled at the vividly described fields of lavender, a purple hue spread for miles on both sides of the road they now traveled. But the time then was in mid-July. Now it was late May. So all he could do was imagine the thousands of dormant gray-green plants around them would soon answer Nature's call to reach full bloom and send out their famous perfumed scent.

It was a sparkling morning, around eleven, and because of such surroundings and history, he was in no hurry to arrive at the southern edge of Plateau de Vaucluse, even though he looked forward to seeing its dry-stone fortifications set against the base of cliffs—those that had once provided cover for successful military action.

The monastery known as the Cistercian Abbey Notre-Dame-de-Senanque was hardly what David had expected. It was a sprawling assembly of buildings that were no doubt once separate from one another but, for whatever reasons, became joined. A large number of second-story walkways were a dead giveaway. David counted seven in all as he maneuvered the car into an empty parking area.

They walked slowly toward the dome-topped entrance marked "South Wing", passing no monks or other personnel. The silence was deafening. Even the birds overhead were not chirping. In short, the place seemed deserted. On the inside ground floor too.

The door was unlocked so they entered without knocking or otherwise announcing their arrival. They found themselves in an immense rotunda-like space with beige masonry walls, uncarpeted oak flooring and dim lighting. There were no furnishings nor wall paintings, and a musty smell was pervasive but not offensive.

David spoke softly: "Where *is* everybody? Off praying? I now know what Paul meant, Musc. Just before we hung up, he said not to be shocked with the place. That it was a bit creepy and reminded him of an old-time horror film."

"Good observation," Musco said.

Suddenly, an elderly man came limping through the only other door in sight. He was neatly dressed in a gray upper garment, matching moccasins and black flannel pants. Clean-shaven and bald, he carried an oversized notebook.

"You must be …let's see …Dr. David Brooks and …Mr. Musker Diller," he said, referring to his notes.

"That's Musco," David said.

"I beg your pardon. These glasses aren't very good."

"But you're not wearing any," Musco remarked.

"I'm not? Well, there's the answer. No-good glasses are better than none at all."

His laugh echoed throughout the rotunda.

"Well, regardless, you're here," the man said. "Let me introduce myself. I'm Frère Rudolph. You know, like the reindeer. I'm the sub-prior here. Frère Dominic is upstairs in the library, waiting for you. Have you ever met him?"

"No," David said. He was tempted to add: "Have you?" but didn't think it would go over very well.

Rudolph led them upstairs to a small library, then left after saying he would be of service if needed.

In the library, an even older looking man sat in an oversized chair, reading. He carefully raised his head and said in a soothing voice: "Yes, you've come, David and Musco. Welcome! Welcome to Senanque." His body trembled slightly as he rose to shake hands, and asked that his honorable visitors—as he called them—sit near him so they might converse.

He was tall and wrinkled with sunken cheeks. "I am Frère Dominic," he said, "but everyone calls me Dom, so please do. In case you haven't already heard, I've been here over 60 years and it's time to leave, which I'll do after Christmas, if I make it till then. So I'm doubly fortunate that you've decided to come now, even though the lavenders haven't yet cast their glow on us."

He was as neatly dressed as Rudolph, but his appearance was marred by strands of unruly white hair which he played with as he spoke.

The library itself was impressive. Book shelves sprouted from every inch of available spacc, filled-to-the-brim.

After thanking the prior for receiving them, David said, "Looks like you have here all the books known to man."

"Not quite, but I'm over 90 now and I've been reading for a long time. I'm almost through collecting, I'm afraid."

"Dom—you're sure I can call you that?"

"I wouldn't have it any other way."

"Well, Dom …before we get started on our mission, may I ask two irrelevant questions?"

"Yes, please do."

"One, where *is* everybody?"

"They're all praying down the hall, in our auditorium. Not in our largest chapel—it's too small to accommodate them. Although we have a total of ten chapels, we wanted our staff to be all together. And I'll get to why they're praying in a little while."

"I see. And my second question is: this entire structure we're in—it's magnificent, by the way. But it was split up at one time, I take it?"

"Yes, and attaching the separate buildings was my idea—30 years ago. I believed that joining our various departments was a sign of unity. Just like our staff now who are praying together. And our histarians—you know all about them by now—we're united in seeking the truth and dispensing it to the proper people."

"'Proper people' meaning who?"

"Like you. Like those we trust. Those poor souls in danger and needing help. Those recommended by other histarians."

By then, David, more relaxed in his chair, felt it

was the appropriate time to address the reasons they had made the trip.

But he was preempted by the prior who said: "Now getting to why they're all praying—and I'd be in there too except I was awaiting your arrival. I'll return though, as soon as we finish here. But understand, I'm not suggesting that we hurry. The Lord understands.

"In May of each year, we gather together to pray from eight to one every day for a week. It's to ask that the world continue. That the future be unlocked. You've already heard me refer to my own demise. That would be nothing compared to the demise of humanity.

"And I must insert here that what I'm saying and what I will shortly say bear on important information I want you to know about. It's information that has become, whether you realize it or not, part and parcel of your investigative work, David. You'll see."

David's relaxation was short-lived.

The prior continued. "You saw me reading a book when you came in. It's called *Ancient Secrets of the Bible. Investigating the Mysteries of Scripture.*"

He picked up the book and ran it before David and Musco.

"I want to read you something from it and when I get to the part that applies to you and your current obligations, I'll let you know. It's two words. But really, the whole three or four paragraphs apply. The two words and their meaning have to do with someone you know and who represents a deadly threat, possibly to all of humanity."

Once again, David fingered his decision scar, but said nothing more than, "Let's have it."

> Images of angels descending, great trumpets sounding, terrifying judgments being unleashed, people standing before a great white throne of judgment—the Bible's depiction of the end boggles the mind. Undoubtedly, these images seem strange and mysterious to most readers; but whatever we make of them, at least one thing can be discerned: someday, God will make the final judgment on right and wrong.
>
> To the first-century men and women who encountered the writing and proclamation of the Early Church, Jesus' promise to return, called the Second Coming, carried with it the hope that justice would be done and faith rewarded.
>
> However, the precise events surrounding the end are shrouded in secrecy. Perhaps no other biblical subject generates as much curiosity and debate as the "end times."

When—and how will the end come about?

"'End times' are the two words?" David asked.

"No. Before that. 'Second Coming'."

"I'm not quite clear, Dom."

"This will take some explaining, I'm afraid. I'll see if I can do it without leaving anything out. First of all, do appreciate that because of Nadim Maloof, Thatcher Drinkwell and other histarians they've kept contact with, I'm aware of all you're going through, including murders, situations, threats, circumstances and people. I can even name the people. I'll name the pivotal one in a few minutes. And if I forget, please remind me to cover arsenic and the Napoleonic era. But I doubt I'll leave those out because of their bearing on that person.

"Some people believe the end will come through wars. I don't. I believe wars will remain as just a part of history."

Here it comes, David thought. *And all through memory.*

"Speaking of history, there are those who describe me as a 'history buff'. I never liked that designation because people might think I read in the nude, but I suppose that's what I am. As such, I've read about the importance of the Stone Age through developments in ancient Egypt and in the civilizations of Mesopotamia and Sumeria and Babylonia; in the battles of the Hittites and the Persians and the Assyrians; through the glory of Greece and the grandeur of Rome, as they say; and on into the Middle Ages. And I've read and reread the sad details of terrible wars—revolutionary, civil, worldwide; the rise and fall of Hitler and Stalin dictatorships in Europe; anti-colonial sentiment in Africa and Asia; flaming battles for independence in Kenya, Algeria, Mozambique, Angola and Rhodesia; the Mao Tse-tung cultural revolution in China; Israel's six-day war in Egypt; internal turmoil in Russia, Nicaragua and the Philippines; skirmishes in the Falklands and Granada and Northern Ireland; the rise of terrorism and the 9/11 attacks; ethnic cleansing in Yugoslavia; ongoing events in the Middle East.

"That brings me to Napoleon. Some are certain he died of deliberate arsenic poisoning. That it might have been planned and executed by a certain conniving lady named Lady Beckett. She was an official of the East India Tea Company and allegedly carried on an affair with the military genius when he was living as a prisoner on St. Helena. And for whatever reason, she decided to kill him.

"Now let me skip to that person you know—the deadly threat person. Her name is Cristina De la Fuente. From Buenos Aires. I'll give you her pertinent medical history— one she's hidden from just about everybody except Nadim Maloof, her former husband. I know him well because he's our Egyptian histarian. She spent over three months in a mental institution. The doctors couldn't pinpoint a diagnosis. In place of it, they were only able to list certain mental symptoms: regression, fantasy and identification. I'm not an expert on them, but I would say they're self-explanatory. When she fell ill, some people began to say that she may have had a hand in your governor's stabbing and in the shooting of Shiro of Cairo. And if she didn't, she knows who did. Essentially, she began to fancy herself as a modern-day Lady Beckett. As the 'Second Coming' of Napoleon's lover and eventual murderer."

David could hardly believe what he was hearing.

"Who are the 'some people'?" he asked.

"Sorry, David, I can't say. But they were other histarians who don't want their names revealed. And I must respect that."

"Does Thatcher know all this?"

"Yes, that's why he insisted you come here. He doesn't mind my mentioning his name as long as it's to you. And, I'm sure to Musco, there. But Thatcher couldn't tell you himself. He's very strict about what he shares—and with whom."

David shook his head as if to straighten out some thoughts.

"But does that mean Cristina is an histarian, too?"

"Hardly. She learned of the Lady Beckett/ Napoleon possibility from Nadim. He told her all about it. It was at that point when she started to show signs of regression and so on. And, at the same time, she became overly impressed with the story of Lady Beckett."

"So she patterned herself after that person?"

"Yes. Not consciously but unconsciously. She wanted to identify with her and all her doings. She even wore ruby jewelry as Beckett did."

David was spellbound.

By now, the prior was twisting his hair in more then one place.

"Next," he said, "I'll combine arsenic, the Japanese and the end of mankind as we know it. And may I remind you that I'm aware of your conversation with the two Japanese men after Nadim's lecture in Cairo. I think there's little doubt that the foolishness about candy was just that: foolishness. The same for the other foodstuffs that Nadim lectured about. Those men were trying to hide the word 'arsenic', and their real purpose was in attempting to seek future counsel from Nadim about certain aspects of …not bio-engineering …or candy-engineering …but *arsenic-engineering*. Inhaling arsenic with the very expensive CR-23 added to it."

Dom waited before continuing, apparently to observe the reaction of his two guests.

"The Japanese connection," David said. "Can you expound on that a little more?"

"Only to a degree, because Nadim is more of an authority on it than I am. Remember, he's friends with the Yakuza element in Japan and can use them to supply information. But I would mention to you, here and now, two things: one, that those men from Tokyo said something very revealing when they admitted they represented a substantial number of their countrymen. And two, the use of arsenic is what I'm afraid could end the world, depending on the size of their target. I don't think we're talking about something like sarin in subways. In any event, I'd contact Nadim directly. There may be more developments."

"And getting back to Cristina," David said. "She's part of this whole conspiracy?"

"I wouldn't put anything past her, including mass extinction. She has it in for Nadim; as I said, she may have killed that Shiro fellow and even your governor; and she has a history of mental imbalance. I may be wrong, but the fact she's able to hide 'the second coming of Lady Beckett' is very significant. Those mental aberrations of hers may still run very deep, and instead of mimicking Beckett's role in Napoleon's death, she may very well prefer to help in the death of not *one* man but of *all* men. And women."

If David had imagined what the assignment would entail, before being asked to take on the Radford case 17 days ago, he would have refused. He never would have believed he'd be shocked over the extent of what he had learned from a frail-looking prior in a small library, in a monastery, in a tiny village he'd once read about, in southeastern France.

He now presumed that Dom was waiting for a

response to the additional characterization of Cristina, but during that brief interval, David was considering bringing up the subject of the remaining dagger. *But enough is enough*, he thought. Thatcher had said to forget thinking about it, something David couldn't do. Not completely.

"Well, Dom," he said, "it's time for us to leave. We can't thank you enough for your information about the trials and tribulations we face and for sharing it with us."

"But can't you stay a little longer? It's a delight having you here. Wouldn't you like some tea or coffee?"

"No, really. We must be going."

Musco was evidently of the same opinion for he and David rose simultaneously.

"Well, so be it," the prior said. "Good luck, and I'll remember you in my prayers."

"We appreciate that. God is good."

"All the time," Musco added.

David hugged the aged prior ever so gently.

Musco followed suit.

Chapter 15

Conversation was practically non-existent on the way back to Avignon. Musco drove this time, David immersed in thought. About what was now history—and what lay ahead. About his usual line of work, and how much he missed it. But most of all, he missed Kathy, and he promised himself to spend more time with her, whether at home in a quiet setting or at their favorite restaurant, *The Stone House*. The background noise would upset him when they walked in, but it never did after a wine or two.

The R.A.F. plane landed at Hartford's Bradley International Airport, having taken much less time to cross the Atlantic than a commercial plane. It was early afternoon, U.S. time, and David decided to call Kathy at her office.

"At last," she said, exhaling in relief. "Where are you?"

"Bradley. I'll be there in an hour, and I miss you."

"I'm glad because I've missed you, too. Terribly. The worry over what's gone on made me miss you more. I love you, you know."

"I know. In fact it's probably the only thing I know for sure."

"What does that mean? The trip wasn't worth it?"

"No, just the opposite. The prior said some unbelievable things and I'm now confused about what to do. Gomez, Nadim, Paul. I've got to contact them. That I *do* know. But I'll explain when I get there. And Kathy?"

"Yes?"

"Why worry when I'm at a religious monastery?"

"It wasn't that. I guess it's a combination of things. Like you're confused over what to do next, and I'm worried over your confusion. Oh, now *I'm* confused. Does that make any sense?"

"I guess so. You want to hear some details?"

"No, not yet. Later. And look," she said, "I'll soon be caught up with my work for the day, so I'll leave for home within the hour. I'll see you there, not here. I have a surprise for you."

When David arrived home, Kathy was standing just inside the front door, arms straight at her sides. She was wearing a red cashmere wrap cardigan sweater with a plunging neckline and a black sequin miniskirt. But no shoes. And her hair was combed down over her shoulders, framing her face. Her mouth was slightly ajar and he felt stimulated by the subtle fragrance of his favorite perfume.

"Whoa!" he exclaimed. "What's that you're wearing—or not wearing?"

"How did you know there's nothing underneath?" she said huskily.

"That's not what I meant, but I'm glad to hear it."

Kathy snuggled up close, planted a wet kiss on his lips, and whispered, "Want to mess up our bed?"

He carried her to the stairs and halfway up, she said, "I can't wait, Clark."

"Clark?"

"Clark Gable."

David, never breaking stride, responded, "Well, if that's who I am, then you must be Vivien Leigh …no, impossible …you're prettier."

Twenty minutes later, he was less confused and she was less worried.

They headed for their adjoining closets, and Kathy said, "Let's go out for dinner, darling. I didn't keep up with the groceries while you were gone."

But his mind was still on their bed.

He kissed her on the forehead while they were dressing and, with a tinge of innocence, said, "You had this all planned, didn't you?"

"Of course. Something had to keep me going. No kidding, David. I was really worried this time."

The exterior of the *Stone House* never failed to impress them, as did its menus. So much so that they'd rarely dined elsewhere for the past 15 years. They'd never been disappointed with the restaurant's brick oven, wood-fired meals. Not that they ate out that often, maybe once a month, but it always seemed to take on the significance of a special occasion. In David's opinion, it was certainly better than unpacking while, at the same time, trying to digest all the information the prior had furnished him. Better to digest a large Italian meal for a change.

He had dropped his luggage near the front door at home and was determined not to move it until the morning. He also vowed to refrain from thinking about the Radford Business and its many ramifications until the following noon. But he knew himself best and believed that vows were meant to be broken, so he settled on returning to his assignment first thing in the morning. Several phone calls had to be made.

The one-story shell of *The House*, as they referred to it, was light yellow in color and made of stone. It was oval in shape with numerous round-topped recesses, patterned after an ancient amphitheater. They always paused at the front entrance to read an inscription etched into a wooden shield toward the side, in case something had changed or been added.

> Made of Ammonitic Jurassic Limestone,
> 1936
> Patterned after the Roman Arena, Verona,
> Italy

They didn't bother to check with the receptionist who was on the phone. Instead they marched straight to their usual corner and sat at one of their usual tables. Not opposite each other, but side by side. David always insisted on that if they had confidential things to talk about.

On the way, David had recognized many of the other customers and exchanged greetings with those who looked up and didn't have a mouthful. He waved to others.

"Before you say anything," Kathy said, "…I should have delivered a message to you as soon as you got home, but I was preoccupied with you-know-what, and now I remember. Joe Gomez called you every day and wants you to call him back. Says it's very important. He even wanted to know if I could get hold of you and I said I didn't know where you were from one hour to the next. I said your cell phone had been no help and I didn't know when you'd return. He refused to tell me what it was about. So *there*, I delivered the message."

"That's the second thing you delivered in the

last hour."

"David!"

"What?"

"You're right, I did," she said sheepishly.

Milton, their favorite waiter, approached them and took their order of Kendall-Jackson Chardonnay, bread and olive oil.

"And make sure it's 2010, Milt," David said. "I can tell, you know."

"Yes sir, Dr. Brooks. Sorry I made that mistake last time."

"So," Kathy said, barely above a whisper, "here we are and I'm all ears. What was the prior like? A stuffed shirt or what?"

David took out two cards filled with his handwritten notes.

"Not at all," he said. "Very gracious. Old and knowledgeable. Said some scary things, though. Hard to imagine. I'll have to confirm them somehow. But I'll get to that in a minute."

David took a gulp of his wine; Kathy sipped hers.

"The place was nice?" she asked. "I've heard it's beautiful. From Paul, as I recall."

"It certainly is. Probably more so when the lavender blooms in about a month. There must be a million plants in that valley."

"Okay. On with the information," she said, switching to a gulp, herself.

"Well, first off, he had this book, see. It's about some secrets of the bible and he went on to read some paragraphs from it. Can you guess what they were about?"

"How could I? That God was coming to earth any minute?"

"Hey, that's not too far off, Kath. You know the book?"

"No, just a guess."

In that short time, they were beginning to feel the effects of the wine. David more than Kathy. Though his glass was only half-empty, he signaled for another.

"What he said or, rather what the book said, was that the end of the earth is near."

"How depressing And the prior believes it?"

"Yes, if we allow it happen," David said.

"What else?"

"He talked about world history and especially about wars."

"As expected."

"As expected," David said, "but it was all a lead-in to Napoleon Bonaparte and a certain Lady Beckett."

Kathy nudged him with her shoulder. "Wait up, now," she said. "What do wars and Napoleon and that lady have to do with the end of the earth?"

"It was a lead-in to what she said after that. She was his lover but the prior thinks she may have poisoned him with arsenic. And, are you ready for this? Remember that

Cristina De la Fuente?"

"Oh, yes. The kook from Buenos Aires."

"Kook alright. According to the prior, she's a very disturbed person who was once a patient in a mental institution. No real diagnosis but regression and some other things. Mostly symptoms. Some people say—he didn't say who, but you know about histarians, right?"

"Right. They're very close-mouthed."

"Some more than others. Anyway, some say… I assume other histarians… that when she got sick, she might have become part of the scheme to murder Radford and that Shiro guy. Or at the least, she knows the killer or killers."

David had reached his second glass.

"Kath, I'm feeling kinda tipsy," he said, "so stop me if I sound crazy. But I've saved the best for last. Cristina apparently researched Lady Beckett, began to idolize her in a psychotic sort of way, and then thought of herself as a reincarnation of her. Like the 'Second Coming' of Napoleon's lover. So she secretly took on that role."

"Amazing!"

"These things happen. When I was in practice, I knew of some cases almost as bad."

"But not of this… this… what's thc word? Magnitude?"

"I'd have to admit that, but the point is psychotics are hard to predict. I thought she bordered on being one when we met, and after hearing the prior's story about her, I now have no doubt."

The waiter returned and they placed matching orders: shrimp parmigiana.

"You want me to go on, Kath? There's more." He turned over his first card.

"Absolutely. Whatever you remember."

"Well, these notes help. Let's see: the arsenic and Japanese bit. We've both heard about it already, but it's good to have it repeated by someone like Frère Dominic. He said the two guys in Cairo and a large Japanese contingent in Tokyo were, in effect, plotting to use inhaled arsenic either in parts of the world or everywhere. Arsenic bolstered by that expensive CR-23. He advised me to contact Nadim. He said the Egyptian knows more about it than he does, and might even be able to explain the Yakuza's role in the plot, if any."

David turned over both cards several times. "Then the last thing I have here is something I wrote down, as much word-for-word as I could. In fact, the prior saw what I was doing and, bless his heart, slowed down what he wanted to say about that 'second coming of Lady Beckett.' See? Crazy. Right? Not the prior… Cristina. Anyway, here's what he gave me the time to write down:

> Her mental aberrations may still run very deep. Instead of mimicking Beckett's role in Nap's death, she may prefer to help kill not one man but <u>all</u> men and women."

Kathy appeared totally stunned.

Their meals arrived and they ate less deliberately than usual. David had drunk two wines, Kathy one. And he commented that medical authorities recommended these differing amounts for men and women.

He handled the bill with a credit card and as they rose to leave, Kathy wrapped her hand around his wrist and said: “You think you can stay home for a while now? At least in Connecticut?”

“Hope so. Just like my saying that medical research should slow down because every important thing’s already been recorded—and someone just has to make it all gel—well that’s my feeling about the Radford Business et cetera. Certain things have to gel.”

“Certain things?” Kathy said, releasing his wrist. “Like what?”

“I’m not sure yet, but you’ll be the first to hear about them, my love.”

PART THREE:

MISSING

Chapter 16

Of the three phone calls David intended to make the next morning, the one to Chief Joe Gomez was uppermost in his mind. Kathy had left for work.

"Joe, it's me, David."

"Hey! You made it back, or are you still there?"

"Where's that?"

"That Helena place."

"No, I'm in Connecticut now. I didn't know I could miss it so much."

"But the trip was worth it?"

"Every bit of it. But Joe, a question or two. Or is this a bad time?"

"No, not at all. Shoot."

"Anything at your end about the Shiro murder?"

"A couple of things. First of all, as you predicted,

David, the autopsy showed a .22 bullet lodged near the inner table of his skull. The pathologist said it had moved around a lot in the brain. And second, just about all our forensic guys concluded the odor in the hotel room was from perfume—not after-shave as one of them thought––but probably a woman's perfume."

"And I've been thinking, Joe, that Rosa gal in the Pink House—is she trustworthy?"

"Yes. I've known her for years."

"So no chance she might have made off with the dagger?"

"No chance. Really."

"And that former Evita guard. Trustworthy?"

"Same thing—yes."

"So his saying he gave the pair of daggers to Cristina was correct in your opinion?"

"Yes."

"Sorry, just trying to piece things together. At this stage, it's like connecting the dots. Know what I mean?"

"Only too well. Putting two and two together."

David would have continued even if Gomez hadn't known what connecting the dots meant. And for a change, he wanted to *inform* instead of *being informed.*

"You should be aware," he said, "that I have it on reasonable authority our lovely Cristina is a very sick and dangerous lady."

"Not surprised. It's probably why that Nadim fellow

left her."

"Regardless though, were your people able to get fingerprints and a DNA sample from her?"

"Funny you should ask. I got a call from the auction house that she didn't show up there when she was supposed to. Twice. We've been hunting around but we can't locate her. Anywhere."

"Not a trace?"

"None."

"By the way, Joe, after the divorce, did she take up with someone else, as far as you know?"

"It was just rumor, but I believe she did. Poor guy. It was kept under wraps and no one around knows who it might be, or we would have looked into it by now. We're not even sure if they're still at it."

"Any chance the 'he' could be a 'she'?"

"I doubt it. There was never a sign of that kind of thing. And she flirted with men all the time."

David thanked the chief, hung up the phone clumsily, then began to pace. He was burdened with thoughts, some connected, some disconnected. Heading the list were Cristina and Shiro's friend, Jun Hirata, the other Japanese man he'd met after Nadim's Cairo lecture.

Instinctively, he called the chief back. "It's me again. I forgot to ask you about a couple of other things. But before that, I'm not bothering you too much, am I?"

"Don't sweat it, my friend. Call any time. You've certainly helped *me* through the years. And don't forget, we have a mutual case on our hands—Shiro of Cairo. Remember?"

"Hmm . . . that reminds me. Ever hear anything about his cohort, a guy named Jun Hirata?"

"Can't say I have. And I think my colleagues here would have told me if he tried to contact us."

"Strange, isn't it? I would have thought he'd try to locate Shiro by now. They seemed close when I met them, so you'd think Shiro would have told him where he was going and why."

"You're right," Gomez said. "Looking for Evita's belongings. And who knows, maybe even the dagger."

Something suddenly dawned on David: *How did Shiro know I had anything to do with Buenos Aires?* The Chief said the guy claimed he was there on my behalf.

But he dismissed the thought as quickly as it had presented itself.

"The reason for my last question, Joe, is Cristina and her disappearance. You should be aware that I too will be checking on where she might be. I'll be calling Paul D'Arneau. He's a friend of mine, a professional treasure hunter but lately more of a criminal investigator. And I completely trust him. There's that word again. Then I'll be conferring again with Nadim. Maybe he or Paul might have some ideas."

"Speaking of trust, David, do you trust Nadim?"

"Yes, once I learned he's an histarian."

"A what?"

"You don't know about them? But why should you?"

After David had given the lowdown on all the histarians he knew, the Chief said, "We could use one down here. Might make my life easier."

"I'll go ahead and mention it to a certain person. Or at least I'll find out if there's already one in your area. Some of them like to operate secretly and give out their findings only if it's done in a confidential or anonymous way."

"Who's the certain person if I may ask, or is that confidential?"

"The one in Helena, as you call it."

"He's the boss?"

"Not the boss, but his recommendation counts plenty."

"Plenty to you?"

"No, to other histarians."

Gomez took his time following up on the comment. "In other words," he said, "to be one, you have to pass muster. Isn't that a good way to think of it?"

"The *best* way. And I would bet that an histarian serving a man in your position could mean a lot, both to you and the histarian cause."

The reason David chose to prolong such a conversation was because he figured an Argentine histarian could play a key role in finding Cristina. Not now, necessarily; not during the duration of the

Radford Business, but somehow in the future. For he was beginning to separate the Hartford murder from the specter of a world-ending catastrophy.

And who knows? he thought. *Cristina may be missing indefinitely and the Chief, with his many new reliable contacts—courtesy of the histarian—might finally find her. An important find because a woman with an ailment like hers could continue to cause trouble for years, if not generations, to come.*

They both rested the case before David said: "Now Joe, my last question: Do you know if Cristina has or had a favorite place to vacation?"

The silence that ensued confounded David.

Finally Gomez said, "Well, I'll be . . ."

"You'll be what?"

"I never even gave it a thought. She might be there."

"Where?"

"Colonia, in Uruguay. She always bragged about the location. Beautiful place, facing us from across the Rio de la Plata. She ferried there regularly—takes less than an hour. Even bragged about its Radisson Hotel. Gave her big discounts I hear. I'll check it out and get back to you, David."

Chapter 17

David next phoned Paul, saying he'd like to talk about Saltanban, Cristina, the dagger, the prior, Thatcher Drinkwell, Gomez and the Shiro murder.

"Another murder?"

"Yeah, but I'll get to that last."

"Fair enough," Paul said as if they were about to engage in a business deal. But at the same time, David pictured him as open-eyed and ears agog.

Paul requested that David repeat the subjects while he wrote them down. David complied by referring to his own list that had been scribbled on a card.

"I'll start with the prior," David began. "Frère Dominic. Everything you indicated about him panned out: long-winded, the war listing and so forth. But he was most helpful and gave me information I had no idea about, especially about a certain Cristina De la Fuente, her background and her belief about the end of the world."

David then detailed the entire Cristina story. "She said the end of the world, Paul."

"But you just said she was diagnosed as crazy."

"Yes, I did, but having met her …well let's just say she's hard to evaluate. And she's hard to get out of my mind."

"There're probably lots of things jumping around in that mind these days."

"Don't remind me. Jumping and doing summer-saults. For example, I mentioned Gomez and the Shiro murder? As I said, I'll cover it later, but what bothers me is that he said—that's Chief Gomez of the Buenos Aires Police—he said that this Japanese Shiro guy showed up at the department saying he was there on *my* behalf. My behalf! And the question in my mind is: how did he know I was in any way connected with the Chief and that city?"

"You've mentioned before about being tailed?"

"Yes."

"Probably more than you were aware of. And there you have it, David. You're moves aren't secret. You may think some are, but they're probably not …not at this stage. And probably the Japanese are behind it all. Think about it. This fellow Shiro gave it away when he announced your name down there."

David took it as logical advice and was about to say so when Paul changed the subject: "Now, how about Saltanban?"

"Haven't heard from him lately. And between you and me, I don't care to."

"Don't blame you. He may be dried toast right now."

"And the dagger?"

"Gone. Can't locate it, but we tried."

"Who's we?"

David felt his friend's questions were penetrating, but in the best sense of the word.

"Gomez and me. And speaking of the dagger, Thatcher Drinkwell pretty much lectured me on forgetting about it. It's now unimportant, he said."

"And you say?"

"I say he's wrong. It depends on *where* we find it, if we find it at all. If we don't find it and everything gets solved and rectified, then he's right."

"Ah, Drinkwell. What did you think overall?"

"Overall, a decent guy. Just like the prior: very well meaning and helpful. I got a kick out of the components. But they work for him. And whatever works …well, you know."

David even mentioned the Japanese stranger on the Argos boat.

"See," Paul said, 'tailed.' Now, Cristina—but you

covered it already. A complicated mess that's coupled with the Japanese poisoning issue—the targeting and all that. Do you believe it?"

"Paul, it's too threatening not to."

"I suppose that's the safest way to look at it, but I'm just wondering how serious the Japanese are."

David believed that comment revolved around the words "check" and "double-check". He recalled talking to Drinkwell about an arsenic attack and thinking he should double-check such a possible disaster. His meeting with Frère Dominic was the first check. This was the second. But the ultimate one would involve his visiting Japan and speaking with key people there. Or, alternatively, to meet with Harry Shapiro, the journalist with *The New York Times*—the man Drinkwell had mentioned. Shapiro had lived in Japan for several months and had written an article about the subway sarin attacks.

David decided to turn to another subject for a moment. He summarized everything he could recall about Gomez and the Shiro murder. Paul listened, apparently absorbed, but at the end, commented little. Instead, he repeated what he'd said ten minutes before.

"I'm just wondering how serious the Japanese are. Don't forget, if they're hinting at …I even hate to say it …the end of the world, it means the same for them personally. No, my view is that they're aiming high, but would be shooting low."

"Or somewhere in between."

"Not even that, because it might take some of them out, too. But no matter their target, we've got to head them off."

David tried to comprehend what the most plausible target might be.

"Your best guess then is something more localized, like here in Connecticut?"

"Yes. And another thing. To follow through with the whole world—do you realize what that would entail? The kind of organization it would require? What, almost 200 countries? We would have heard …or you would have heard about it from all your worldwide histarians by now."

"And that hasn't happened."

If you say so, but it's an important thing for you to investigate."

"Of course. I'll get right on it. It's called mushrooming."

"Meaning?"

"I ask my favorite histarians if they've heard anything about it. They in turn ask their favorite ones, and so on. Soon, hundreds and hundreds are asking around or doing pertinent research."

"That's exactly what's needed."

David was near describing his most recent experience with such a process, one involving the kidnapping of an armed bank guard, when he decided to back off. He believed he had rehashed the essentials of mushrooming.

"But this is so one-sided," he said.

"I don't understand."

"The subject matter. Do you ever think about our other calls to each other, say a month ago or before that?"

"Often. The case either one of us was working on at the time in contrast to what we're facing now."

"You mean *I'm* facing—but you've reacted as though you're just as involved, and I'm grateful for that, Paul."

"There may come a time when the situation is reversed, and I know you'd do the same for me."

"You can count on it. Anything overwhelming for you now?"

"I'm ashamed to bring it up. How does the disappearance of an heirloom sound as compared to the disappearance of mankind?"

"But yours is real. Mine is at the threat stage."

Over the phone, Paul's thinking almost had a sound to it. "David, here's what I suggest: stop traveling far and wide; consider your principle challenge the one you were hired to face—solving the governor's murder; don't minimize the Japanese issue but don't lose sleep over it. There's just so much a single person can do, even you. The Japanese men said they were in no hurry and neither should you be. Take things a day at a time, get your rest, show your love for Kathy, keep your responsibilities in order and call me whenever you feel the need."

The need David felt right then was to give his friend a bear hug. And he would have if he'd received the encouragement in person.

Chapter 18

David was about to place his last call for the morning. It was approaching ten in the United States, no doubt dinnertime in Alexandria. But his phone rang.

"David? Joe Gomez here."

"That didn't take long. What did you find out?"

"Cristina hasn't been to Colonia's Radisson in months. I even asked to speak with the manager there–guy named Chico. I'd heard they had something going whenever she showed up, and he said she hasn't been there since before Christmas."

"Maybe that's why she always chose *that* place."

"How's that again?"

"Their 'thing'."

"Oh, yeah—little slow this morning. You can bet he's not the only one."

"Too bad we can't speak to any of them. Maybe we'd learn a lot."

"I'm not sure about how to go about it, but I'll try to dig up what I can and get back to you again. Maybe I'll check with Chico, although he may not want to talk about it."

"On the other hand, he may be pissed that she doesn't show anymore and would be more than happy to say why."

"That someone else came along?"

"Precisely. Is he married?"

"I'm not sure."

"Were he and Cristina serious?"

"Not sure of that either, but I doubt it."

David was pondering as they spoke. Finally he said, "What you might do, Joe, is check with all the other hotels there. How big is the town?"

"About twenty-five thousand."

"Shouldn't be too hard. Can you enlist others over there to help out?"

"Good idea and that's how I'll handle it. I might even have them check with real estate agents. She's maybe worth some money by now, especially if she charges."

"I wouldn't put it past her," David said. "She probably equates it to being a savior of some sort."

"Like in saving money?" Joe responded. " …ooh, that was bad."

"Not really," David said. "Anyway, let's keep

in touch."

Among David's first words to Nadim were: "I hope I'm not being too blunt, but why didn't you tell me you're an histarian?"

"You *know* then. The answer is that the less the number of people who are aware of it, the more I accomplish. For some of my counterparts, it makes no difference. For others, they're like me—working in the dark, so to speak."

"Well, I was pleased to hear it. I can call on you if I need help in your area?"

"Not only around here, but anywhere. There are many of us and we often operate as a unit."

"Good. I'll remember that."

"As long as you brought it up, may I ask who told you?"

"Thatcher Drinkwell. He probably believed I already knew. Don't hold it against him. Please."

"Of course not. Good old Thatcher. But you yourself won't tell anyone, will you?"

"You have my word."

After a moment of thought, Nadim said, "You know, David, several of us have talked about getting *you* to join our ranks. You'd be terrific at it."

"I know. Not that I'd be terrific, but that there's been some discussion about it. That's what I was told."

"By Thatcher, right?"

"Right. And I'll give you the same answer I gave him. I'd be honored, but my plate is just too full to squeeze anything more on it. Maybe someday when I slow down."

"Too bad. We could use you, what with all your connections—your experience. So, slow down."

"Thanks, Nadim. We'll see. And whether I'm an histarian or not, call if I can ever help—without breaking a confidence, of course. And tell your cohorts the same thing, only in that case, *you* call me first to verify who might be contacting me. You understand, don't you?"

"Yes, of course."

"Now the reason I called is twofold, maybe threefold or more. And I hope none of it's too personal. Who initiated your divorce? Any idea where Cristina is or could show up? Something about the Japanese Yakuza. And something about the remaining dagger."

"Fine. First, I started the divorce proceedings once I became aware of her mental condition and behavior. You know all about that, don't you?"

"Yes, I do. Frère Dominic went into great detail. Unreal story."

"Sure is. And second, I have no idea where she is. You've lost track of her?"

"Yeah, completely, I'm afraid."

"Sorry to hear it. She could be a menace, wherever she is. Or better put, wherever she strikes."

"I'd agree with that, so do let me know if you receive

even a hint about her location. What state? What city? Even what country? If it's another country, that's when I might be tempted to contact your colleagues."

"I'll keep my eyes and ears open, David. And the Yakuza?"

"I heard you talk about your relationship with them during the Cairo lecture, and I completely understand. But could you inquire about what they might know regarding a Japanese element gearing up for a widespread arsenic attack. Or even a narrow-spread, if there is such a word?"

"I'd be glad to. I don't know many of them but the one I'm most familiar with—I'm sure he'd cooperate. So, to boil it down, you want to know if such an attack is hearsay, plain bluster, or really in the works."

"That's correct," David said, as if responding to a court attorney. "And last: the dagger. You undoubtedly know what my question is."

"Do I know where it might be? And the answer is no, not at all. But I also have a suggestion."

"What's that?"

"Forget about it. I've given it some thought—naturally—and I came to the conclusion that it wouldn't change anything even if it's found."

"This is getting creepy. That's exactly what Thatcher said. I didn't defend my position on it at the time, but I will now. What if it turns up in Cristina's possession—if we find her?"

"So?" It was said in a conciliatory tone.

"She told one of Eva Perón's former guards that she wanted to auction it off—along with the other one used to kill our governor—and donate the money back to the Musea Evita."

"Again, so?"

"I just think that if that didn't happen …and it didn't …it has some significance. Maybe she now feels it could somehow be used as evidence against her in some way. I mean if she took part in the murders. And therefore she doesn't want anyone else to have it."

"I see the reasoning, but don't forget, she's crazy."

After some concluding small talk, each agreed to notify the other with any news, good or bad.

David continued sitting at his desk, grappling with reasonable moves he could make, all based on the phone calls just concluded. He'd learned plenty from them, more than he expected.

Chapter 19

Harry Shapiro of *The New York Times* was next.

David opened the bottom drawer of his desk and removed the card that Drinkwell had given him. There were five recommendations listed and two of them concerned Shapiro—one about seeing the journalist in person, and the other about Shapiro's possibly writing another article on Japan, one that might deal with the Japanese threat. A flash point or a sham? David felt that a person in his position would be a straight shooter.

When he had first read the card in the constable's St. Helena office, David interpreted the part about an arsenic attack as a definite. But all indications since then had reduced it to a possibility. The three-sentence, fourth recommendation was worded: "The scheme must somehow be brought out into the open. Let others do it. Maybe Shapiro can write another article in *The Times*."

David phoned the paper and had no trouble reaching Shapiro. Following a mutual admiration dialogue, David asked if they might meet halfway between Hollings and New York for a most meaningful discussion.

"It concerns some worries I have about what might be up Japan's sleeve," he said.

"I'd be glad to. As you may or may not know, Paul D'Arneau and I have become good friends and call each other from time to time. And he's already brought me up to date about the whole Japanese tale …if I might label it as such. Last time we met was at the Yale library. How would that be?"

"Good choice. I graduated fromYale, you know."

"Yes, I do. So you're familiar with the Linconia and Brothers Room at the Sterling Library?"

"Very much. Spent a good deal of time in there—nice and quiet."

"And private, if we make it so. I can take care of that."

"Meet you there then at, say, one-thirty?"

"Perfect."

The drive to the library was one in which David forced himself to be free of disturbing ideas, hoping that the upcoming meeting would thus be more fruitful. He was only partially successful, as a steady diet of conflict and distraction was too much to overcome. It was a relatively cool afternoon, low hanging clouds blurring the boundary between earth and sky.

Their designated meeting room was one of six that formed a first-floor wing of the library. David found it unoccupied. On the far side, four casement windows opened onto a courtyard. There was a window seat below and scattered about were several groupings of tables with lamps and a large center table with green leather chairs.

He sat near the end of the large table and placed Friday on the carpeting near his side, having stuffed some pertinent papers in it before leaving Hollings.

Soon, a man resembling James Cagney walked in and introduced himself as Harry Shapiro. He took a seat opposite David. He too had a briefcase, but he placed it on the table and emptied it of its contents: five folders brimming with sheets of paper, several envelopes and two newspapers.

As David viewed him, Shapiro was actually a cross between the movie actor and Sparky, with black hair parted in the middle, probing blue eyes and a prominent forehead. He removed a brown-checked jacket slung over a shoulder and draped it over the emptied briefcase before placing both on the floor.

David broke the ice saying: "So you're an histarian, I'm told."

"Yes, and you should be one, too."

"No, not you, too!"

"Why not? You'd be great."

"We'll see. Just too busy right now." David wanted to get off the subject. "I can't thank you enough for taking the time to drive here," he said.

"My pleasure. It's always good to escape the hustle and bustle of *The Times*. And, of course, to meet with someone of your reputation."

"Hmm, you may change your mind before we're through …may I call you Harry?"

"Uh-huh. And I can call you David?"

"Please do. Anyway, you know why we're here, and frankly, I don't know where to begin."

"I'll make it easy for you." Shapiro removed some papers from two of the folders and spread them in front of him, much as Thatcher Drinkwell had. "I'll tell you what I told Paul as best I can and you pick out what you think is important. Stop me at that point, and I'll clarify or elaborate."

"Fair enough. You've got plenty of material there."

"For sure. The moment I started at *The Times*, my boss said to keep background records of every article I wrote, mainly because of possible lawsuits."

The journalist removed a news clipping that was lodged in one of the folders. Then, taking his pencil, he carefully underlined some sentences on most of the papers on the table. He waved the clipping in the air, saying, "Here's the piece I did about Japan, so I'll be moving back and forth between it and these sheets here.

And if I sneak a peek at the other folders now and again, I hope it won't be a distraction to you. Also, in addition to stopping me when you want, please don't hesitate to take notes. You didn't take along a recorder, did you?"

"No. I probably should have." Already, David was impressed with Shapiro's style.

"Tomorrow I'll write an article you might be happy with. Then, I'll make it my business to have it appear in the next edition of our paper, and send copies to my journalistic buddies near and far, requesting them to have it show up in *their* papers."

"Harry, you've really got this organized." David didn't know what else to say.

"I hope so. I even have the opening few words: 'In Japan, there's talk about . . .' and so on and so forth."

Shapiro lowered his head, ran his fingers across his eyebrow, and looked back up.

"I'll do my best to couch the language so that, on the one hand, the bad guys know we're well aware of what they might be up to, and that we're ready to counteract it. And on the other hand, so we don't scare the general public. I think this approach will go a long way in handling the problem. What do you think so far?"

"It couldn't be better."

Shapiro took out a bottle of water from his briefcase and downed nearly half of it. "So, let's begin," he said. "Don't forget—it will be fairly much what I said to Paul, so if you've heard it before—from him—I apologize."

“No need to. The more I hear it, the better.”

“The extremist group that organized and implemented the 1995 sarin release in Tokyo was called Aum Shinrikyo, and still is. It’s also known as Aum and Aleph and is a Japanese cult that combines tenets from Hinduism and Buddhism, and they’re absolutely obsessed with the apocalypse. It was a simultaneous attack on five trains in the subway system that killed 12 commuters, seriously injured 54 and caused over 6,000 more to seek medical attention.

“Aum’s founder, Shoko Asahara, claims he’s the first enlightened one since Buddha. At the time of the attack, Aum claimed it had 40,000 members worldwide and had offices in Russia, here in the United States and obviously in Japan. The group eventually split into two factions over a dispute regarding religious beliefs. Asahara, by the way, was constantly predicting that the end of the earth was near and that only his devoted followers would survive.”

Shapiro looked at David’s note pad. “Nothing written, so far?” he asked.

“Not yet. I’ll keep it up here.” He tapped his forehead.

After another slug of water, Shapiro resumed his revelations. “So as far as I can tell, we have a guy like that—Asahara Loony Tunes—still on the loose. And what are they planning? They intend to release a form of arsenic that can be inhaled—somewhere in New York,

Connecticut and Massachusetts. That will be their trial run. If it works to their liking, they'll aim for other areas, both here and abroad. Meanwhile, they say, millions will be panicking—and dying—and that'll give them time to use it everywhere in the world.

"They haven't lost their loyalty to sarin, so they reversed its letters to give the arsenic gas a special name: 'Niras'. Then the group began preaching that Niras is the name of a Buddist goddess!"

David made his first entry in the note pad.

"Now, there's more. There are still some disenfranchised members of Aum in Tokyo. I met some of them while I was assigned there for a spell. Seems as though I talk to one every week, at least. Thatcher tells me he went into this with you, but it bears repeating. They insist that Niras would be more potent and more dispersible if that expensive chemical, CR-23, is added to it. And on top of that, once people start inhaling the combination, they have to continue to do so—just like arsenic. So either way, they die: by inhaling it or stopping it once they start."

"David, I could go on and on about that Inoue…" Shapiro followed along the underlined sentences in his paper. " …about military Islamic extremists; about special operation forces and perimeter security measures that we have in this country; and counter-terrorist forces in Japan. But I think you have your hands full as it is."

"I certainly do, but you've been most helpful and

a good deal of what you say verifies what others have told me."

"Only a good deal?"

"Sorry, I was clumsy. What I mean is I've *heard* a good deal of what you said and that matches what others have told me. As for the new material, there's no reason for me to doubt it."

"Good. And oh …I left out one thing, and you've certainly heard this before, too. The candy and other foodstuff malarkey? Just a cover."

David nodded.

For another 20 minutes, they exchanged stories about mutual histarian friends, before they thanked one another and went their separate ways.

On the drive back to Hollings, David thought that Shapiro had been the ultimate check. And that his willingness to cite names in another article and then to distribute it was a godsend.

Chapter 20

When David returned home from Yale, he received a call from Joe Gomez.

"Mayday, Mayday, Mayday!" he cried, as jubilant as David had ever heard him.

"Yes, it's a day in May, but what's up? You sound like you're about to jump out of your skin."

"The front desk at Colonia's Radisson just called here and guess what?"

"What?"

"Cristina checked in about an hour ago! She's with a guy they've seen her with many times before."

"Hard to believe," David said, trying to curb his excitement. "You going over there?"

"Yes, sir. A couple of us deputies are. Right now."

“Call me back from there, okay. I’ll be at Kathy’s office. I wish I weren’t so far away.”

“Will do. Sounds like she’s really deteriorated, David. Was very open about what she said, like, ‘I’m glad I did it. That Jap deserved what I dished out.’ Things like that.”

“Where’s she been? Did she say?”

“Only that she’s been off praying to Buddha.”

“And her companion—did he give his name?”

“Not really. He registered as John Smith from the States.”

“What did he look like?”

“They said tall, good-looking and, even with the hot and humid weather down here, he was wearing a vest. A red one.”

“Did you say a red vest?”

“Yes, bright red.”

“Bennett?”

“What’s that?

“Nothing. Just thinking out loud.”

David wanted to ask the right questions before passing the news on to Kathy and Sparky. He called her, barely mentioning the call from Buenos Aires, and asked that Sparky be at her office when he arrived there in ten minutes. Besides this unanticipated development, he wanted to bring them up to date on the other phone conversations he’d had earlier.

“So how will you deal with Cristina once you get

there?" he asked Gomez.

"I'll arrest her. She's really dangerous, David."

"And him?"

"I'll arrest him, too, as an accomplice to a potential killer. We can keep him locked up overnight, and I'll hurry all the papers through. Then we'll extradite him there."

"Perfecto, Joe. I'll either be here or at Kathy's office if you need to contact me."

At police headquarters, David gave her and Sparky a rundown of the day's events.

"I think we're much closer to solving this damn case," Sparky said. Kathy nodded her approval.

But it didn't quite work out that way, at least with the man who appeared to be psychiatrist Philip Bennett.

It was early evening when David received another call from Gomez who was then in Colonia. He said the man was nowhere in sight and Cristina was not talking.

"We'll keep stalking out the area and if we find him, I'll call you back."

David, totally distressed, never heard back from the Chief that night, and after conferring with Kathy, he knew what had to be done the next morning.

Promptly at nine a.m., he went to the hospital and found Bennett's office door locked. He then retraced his steps and entered administrator Alton Foster's office.

"Dr. Bennett's not in?" he asked. "He's usually

early, isn't he?"

"Usually, but he's taken most of the week off. What's today anyway—Thursday? He should be in tomorrow. At least that's what he told me."

"I see," David said. "He wouldn't be at home today, by any chance?"

"You can try calling there, but he said he'd be doing some traveling and wouldn't be back till late tonight."

"Does he take much time off?"

"Interesting you should ask. Yes, especially over the past year or so. Some of his patients are even complaining. They have appointments with him, and he doesn't show. He's even missed some Board meetings as you might have noticed. But why do you ask? Is there something wrong?"

"Uh …I can't say wrong for sure …let's just say fishy."

David then checked in with Kathy at police headquarters. When informed of Bennett's absence and that he wasn't expected back for 24 hours, she correctly assumed David would be antsy for most of the day—she'd seen it before.

"Look, darling," she said, "there's nothing you can do about it now. Why not capitalize on it? Go home, read a book, reenergize, get some rest—god, look at you. You could use it."

David complied. He slept on and off for most of the day, but he never reached the point of being reenergized.

The next morning, he found Bennett seated at his desk. The psychiatrist appeared unusually solemn.

"Well," he said, "still wanting a profile of our killer, no doubt."

What a strange comment, David thought. "No doubt."

He wanted to ease into a conversation to see what he might bring out. He eyed a medallion hanging from Bennett's neck and decided that reference to it was a good way to begin. Or he could have complimented him on his bright blue vest. He chose the medallion.

"Tell me, Phil, I've been itching to ask you—that medallion—you wear it a lot. Is it used as a metronome in hypnosis?"

"Precisely."

"Well, keep it still or I'm outa here!"

"Relax, David. Why would I want to hypnotize you? Besides, I'd need your full cooperation."

"So it's still being used for that purpose?"

"It is in *this* office. Better than any new-fangled science, except for what we're doing here now. And that may have to be phased out soon, thanks to our former governor."

David was momentarily speechless, wondering if Bennett's last statements bore any significance. He studied the medallion, tempted to reach over and touch it.

It was triangular in shape. At first glance, its three corners appeared rounded. David estimated the length of each side to be about two inches. Each side featured a row of tiny ivory beads and in the center of the triangle was a corresponding large bead. He was about to change the subject when it suddenly struck home that the right lower corner looked square rather than round. A bead that should have been there was missing. Along with its empty metal cup.

In an instant, David's thinking shot back to the vacuum sweep of the Hartford crime scene: the bead and cup on the filter paper! *Here's our killer!*

He didn't want a confrontation with Bennett so he checked his watch, said he just dropped in to say hello, and left. He headed for Foster's office again.

"Alton," he said, "would I be permitted to look at Dr. Bennett's file?"

"Sure. Why not? After all, you're the Board chairman."

David wanted to explore one specific thing: the psychiatrist's training locations. He found them listed on the front page of his application for medical privileges at Hollings. Bennett had studied in Boston, Japan and Buenos Aires!

In the next corridor, David took out his cell phone and called Kathy. He explained what he'd discovered and asked that she and Chief Medicore come over and immediately arrest the psychiatrist with a charge of first-degree murder.

"And please make it fast," he said. "I left there in a hurry, and he's disappeared on us before."

"So you think he was the man with Cristina?"

"Sweltering weather down there and he's wearing a bright red vest? No question."

Chapter 21

Under aggressive and relentless interrogation, Dr. Philip Bennett admitted that he had murdered Radford. He gave a rambling, convoluted account of his motive. He stated that he became infuriated upon learning that the governor had cut off funding for the consortium, thus torpedoing the mission of the newly formed Hollings Research and Development Center. Bennett's study in both Japan and Argentina had focused on psychiatric research and essentially, he had become a noted scholar in that endeavor—publishing in medical journals, speaking on the subject to national scientific groups, directing the research of others. His dream was to become president of the Psychiatric Society, not of the county or state, but of the entire country. Then after the murder, he switched that dream to one of becoming a hospitalist in order to divert attention away from the former dream that Radford "had dashed to smithereens", as Kathy, one of the interrogators, recorded it.

When questioned about Japan, Bennett said he'd forged certain relationships during his two years of study and research there. And while he didn't agree with the arsenic issue, he sympathized with the country's dismay over helping to underwrite Radford's run for governor, only to be denied future funding for the chemical CR-23 that was produced by a Tokyo firm.

"You can understand my thinking, can't you?" he asked. "I went berserk when I learned what was happening, right before my eyes. My action was justified because of what he did to me and to other people too. In a way, I was acting on their behalf. Please take that into consideration," he pleaded.

"It was an action of intentional murder," countered Chief Medicore who was also at the session. As was David and three attorneys.

The psychiatrist was taken to Somers State Prison to await trial.

Once home, David sat at his desk with a kettle of tea at his side. He phoned Musco, Sparky, Paul, Gomez, Nadim, Thatcher, Frère Dominic and Saltanban, in that order. He informed them of the interrogation result and the steps leading up to it. None of them expressed surprise and only Saltanban registered a complaint of sorts:

“You mean I wasn’t mentioned as a victim, too? I’m just one of the ‘other people’?”

David couldn’t tell whether the snicker he heard was genuine or contrived.

That evening at the *Stone House*, he and Kathy raised their glasses in a toast.

“To justice,” she said.

“And to fatigue,” he added.

EPILOGUE

Dr. Bennett was found guilty of first degree murder and sentenced to life without parole.

Chief Gomez *did* arrest Cristina. She was ruled mentally incompetent to stand trial and was committed to El Borda Psychiatric Hospital in Buenos Aires.

With regard to the second dagger, it was never located. That pleased David because he believed an absent dagger symbolized the frustration of the case.

Before he wound down his efforts for good, he typed up several leftover questions, with likely answers:

1. Why was a Buenos Aires dagger used anyway? Answer: Bennett was convinced that one made there would throw investigators off. He had taken up with Cristina shortly after the divorce from Nadim and visited her often. He had no trouble obtaining the set of daggers.
2. How did the weapons get by customs at the airport? Answer: Bennett said they were of historical value. That, plus *money talks.* He inserted them in his large suitcase,

not his carry-on.

3. What of the black SUV that often teased me? Answer: It belonged to Bennett. I checked in his garage.
4. Who ordered my captivity on the Rock of Gibraltar? Answer: Bennett. He knew nothing of my experience in speleology.
5. Who left the note attached to my windshield wiper? Answer: Bennett again. He was aware of the hospital murders 12 years ago.
6. Why did Radford cancel the funding? Answer: unknown.

Next, David phoned Shapiro back and asked if he would notify the Japanese police and the Japanese Parliament of the case's disposition and of the effort to expose those responsible for the arsenic threat. The journalist heartily agreed to do so and repeated what he had said to David on the previous call: Congratulations for the handling of a case with many seemingly insurmountable ramifications.

Then David spread the word around—what had been accomplished and what to be prepared for—by personally contacting Interpol, The Hague, the United Nations, the White House, the United States Congress, and the Office of Homeland Security.

Within a few days, he returned to his hanging caseload. Once the three had been resolved, he reduced any future investigations to one case at a time. That allowed him the opportunity to become an effective histarian.